# FLAMES' FIRST FRACTION

BOOK #1
EPOCH OF THE FLAMES

SANJANA BALACHANDAR

INDIA • SINGAPORE • MALAYSIA

ISBN 979-8-89133-993-4



All credits for the cover pages of this book as well as the illustrations and images are as follows:

1. Cover pages - Leonardo.ai
2. Image of Freya - Artbreeder
3. Map - Inkarnate
4. Image of dragon - Leonardo.ai

# Dedication

To my readers, thank you for taking the time to read my work.

I truly appreciate it.

Oh, and to Milo (my Golden retriever who reminds me of Fleetfoot from Throne of Glass by Sarah J Maas, every chance he gets.)

# Playlist

1. Niteboi – U.
2. Ofdream – Thelema
3. Le Monde – Richard Carter
4. Mertamorphosis – Interworld
5. Another Love – Tom Odell
6. Don't Let Me Down – The Chainsmokers
7. ...Ready For It? – Taylor Swift
8. I Did Something Bad – Taylor Swift
9. Close Eyes – DVRST
10. Don't Blame Me – Taylor Swift
11. E.T – Katy Perry
12. It Won't Kill Ya – The Chainsmokers
13. Ava – Famy
14. War Of Hearts – Ruelle

15. Empires – Ruelle
16. You broke me first – Tate McRae
17. I Can't Handle Change – ROAR
18. Next to You – Oneheart

EVERMIST
FREYA'S CABIN
Zancedeschia
CORVIDUS' CASTLE

VIRIDESCA

RISTOPHER'S CASTLE

EMERALDA

ALEXANDRITE ACADEMY

artbreeder

# Contents

CHAPTER 1

# Dames - Violet

I was trembling in fear. I had no idea where I was, and I was having an internal panic attack. Breathing heavily, I wasn't sure if fear was the right emotion to be experiencing. Maybe excitement, a rush of adrenaline, maybe even happiness, but was it fear? I couldn't feel my legs. It was fear alright. How did I know? By the tense chest, heavy breathing, and sweat dripping from my face, although I was shivering at the same time.

I started walking, discovering the deep and lush forest filled with gigantic crystals, which looked like emeralds.

But before I could do much Nancy Drew-ing, I was apparently flashed back into the flea market where I was getting wildflowers for Mom. And by 'flashed back,' I mean

I instantly reappeared with a bright light encompassing me, into the flea market.

*Umm, okay, weird. Did I just imagine the entire thing? That doesn't seem right…*

I pinched my arm to make sure I wasn't dreaming; then only did I realize that I was back at the flea market and there was absolutely no point in pinching myself. Whatever. That experience was creepy. I hoped I wasn't coming down with some psychotic mental illness where I hallucinated things.

Anyway, I stopped shaking, and my heart rate slowly returned to normal. Everyone was staring at me. Just super. I basically dropped everything I was doing and ran home in the hopes that my journal could help me digest whatever had happened up until now.

Home wasn't that far away. Actually, let me rephrase what I just said, my house wasn't that far away. That place isn't anything like a home. I knew there was no point in telling my parents what happened; they would only laugh and probably spit in my face. I then concluded that they're going to be mad at me for not buying the wildflowers and that they would probably ask me what happened. There was no way in hell that I was telling them what really happened. I was just going to say I had an epiphany for my school project and had to get it down in my diary before

I forgot. That would work. The dimwits wouldn't know what hit them. Otherwise, I was probably at risk of getting sent to an asylum. Nuh-uh. Not on my watch.

I got home within minutes at the speed that I was running at. The door was open, so I sneaked in and ran up the stairs to my dingy, moist, disgustingly comfortable room. I was so used to living in a pathetic, miserable place that I oddly found comfort in there rather than at some lame old sidewalk at a train station. Yes, I once slept on the sidewalk of a train station when we didn't have any money. That was the only thing we had considered to be the closest to an actual house.

I entered my room and shut the door lightly, grabbing my journal from inside one of the cabinet's hidden doors. I started to quickly jot down the description of the place I was just in. The forest. I also drew a shabby drawing of the crystals and greenery before hiding my journal again.

Cassiopeia, my mom, found out I was home and hiding from her and hollered, "Freya! I'm giving you 10 seconds to show yourself before I beat you to death with this mop!"

Without thinking twice about the second set of bruises I'd have to deal with today, I hastily fled downstairs with a tinge of *shit* in the back of my throat. My mom, with her strawberry blonde hair, plump face and body, saw me and grabbed my hand before slapping it with a thud. I winced slightly in pain. It didn't hurt that much, not after being hit so many times. I was used to it at this point.

"Where are the redbuds, girl?" She yelled at my face before lifting her hand to give me another slap. I stopped her by pulling my hand back and running out the door. I was done with her balderdash. Seventeen years of pain, torture, and, well, pure agony, was enough!

My family and I never really got along. It's been a tough life for me. I sometimes thought that I was adopted because of a singular reason: the way my parents treated me. It was never okay, especially in this modern generation of 2021. Was it really necessary? They treated me like a slave, and sometimes I romanticized it by thinking I was like Cinderella, a princess yet to find her prince. But eventually, that story got old, and I decided I didn't need a prince to save me.

In a nutshell, I was a person who was shy, kind, and innocent even. Forgiving, merciful. But that's all changed now. This story will mostly revolve around my life in the past, and eventually, you'll see what my life looks like now. I started here because this is where everything began. This is where my life truly became **my** life and didn't revolve around my parents.

During 2020, when Covid hit, my life was worse. I was made to do all the work and was sent outside without a mask for all the groceries. I was put in jeopardy. But there were times when I made TikToks (I can cringe at this now), and my parents left me alone for a bit, here and there.

I usually loved to read, write, sleep, and whenever I got the chance, I would play a little bit of basketball with my classmates. This story happened in the beginning of summer vacation in 2021. I really didn't have many friends at the time, and the few friends that I did have rarely cared about me.

I had major anger issues, which caused my parents to get even more of an opportunity to judge, criticize, hate, and hit me. It made no sense. But what could I do? Go to the police? Not an option. My relationship with my dad was worse. He was the type who also had anger issues, guess that's where I got my temper from. So, when we both got angry at each other for some nonsensical reason, he used the fact that he's the elder one to his advantage.

My childhood had been a pain, but not all of it. Some of it was nice. I used to enjoy writing stories and scripts/ dialogues in my journal. I had a dream of getting accepted into Harvard. I always wanted to be a writer. I loved imagining beautiful scenarios; they were always an escape for me. They still are as I recite this story.

Anyway, my dad's name is Nyx. Yes, quite an odd name. Freya Nyx.

Back to the present moment I was talking about: I ran out the door to be 'flashed' back into this beautiful world of Emeralds. Or was it Peridots? I'll never know, I guess. But as much as I was scared again, I was also happy; at least I found an escape from my parents finding me.

Within seconds, however, I was 'flashed' again into another place. And this place had a dark, gloomy environment. I saw a castle, and I was then in the forest surrounding it. This forest was nothing like the other forest I was 'flashed' into (the Emerald one). This was a very antagonizing forest. A little creepy as well, might I add.

My jet-black hair flew behind me because of the strong wind currents. What's going on? Yes. But also, I'm away from my parents so, YES! This was the experience of being a traumatized girl without displaying any external emotions. Well, I wouldn't really say traumatized, more like deeply scared. I don't want to just throw around words I don't even know the meaning of. Maybe I have experienced trauma, just not to the degree that other people go through. I feel sorry for them. I know first-hand what it's like to be misunderstood. Wow, this story got deep fast. I think it's essential you know this much about me to start with; things get much, much more profound as we go further into this story. And trust me, you're going to want to stay for the ride. Because it's one hell of a rollercoaster, and I'm the ride's attendant.

## CHAPTER 2

# Meeting Corvidus

I scrambled for a tree trunk to hide behind. Once I found a trunk large enough, I pulled my hoodie up to cover my flying hair in the wind and basically just took a peek at what was going on, trying to understand where I was.

There were a few guards guarding the entrance to the castle. I noticed them the moment I flashed in. I hid immediately, before they could catch sight of me. I mean, who knows where I was and who they were? They could be dangerous. I tried listening in to the conversation of the guards, but oh wait, they weren't even talking. Just doing their job. Maybe I could have asked them for help. After all, I didn't ask for this; I didn't get here on my own. I was going to take a risk. Was it worth it? What if they thought I was an enemy or something? Freya, trust your intuition, stop overthinking, and just go for it.

I smoothed out my navy-blue hoodie and jeans and walked toward the guards. One of them saw me, a few meters away, and he yelled at the other guard: "Imposter!" I understood the assignment and made a break for it. It looked like he might not have even heard me out before trying to kill me. I started to brainstorm while running even deeper into the forest behind me. *Which is the greater enemy? The forest with great unknowns or the guards who don't know who I am?* I suddenly heard a screech coming from inside the forest. I stopped dead in my tracks. What the hell? I looked back. The guards were catching up to me. Which way, Freya, which way? I turned around, taking my pepper spray, which I had on me at the time, and pointed it toward the guards chasing me. I screamed, "Stay Back!"

(The story of me always carrying Pepper Spray isn't too long. Hear me out. It all started in 6$^{th}$ grade when I was being followed on my way home from school. A hooded guy was on my track and started getting a little too close. I somehow managed to pull his hoodie down so I could catch a look at his face if the police ever needed me to remember. He never ended up hurting me, but the creep gave me an eerie smirk before I punched him in the face. Now that I look back on this memory, I'm quite proud of myself for being confident and brave. Well, ever since, I have always carried pepper spray with me. Every day, no matter what.)

Like they would even listen to a scrawny young girl like me. I didn't know what to do, so I stopped and tried to explain to them what was going on and who I was. "Listen, guys, I'm not who you think I am… I'm just a girl who touched a freaking flower and turned up here thirty minutes later. It's not like I'm your enemy or something… so if you could just tell me where I am, then that would be great!" I smiled awkwardly.

One of the guards dressed in gray and black, who had a weird-looking hat on, came closer, and for each step he took toward me, I took a step back. He said, "We don't know who you are, but we've been told to take whoever comes within 100 feet of the palace to the King, and in this case where the King isn't in town, we got to take you to the Prince."

"Oh, well, that's good. I'll gladly follow you to the castle. So, I can talk to him? Maybe ask him where I am and how to get back to Sugar Hill, New Hampshire?"

The guard laughed, tilting his head back. "You aren't from around here, are you?"

I tilted my head. "I literally just said I'm from New Hampshire. And this doesn't look like Sugar Hill to me. It's a small town, I've discovered pretty much every nook and cranny of it."

"This is Zantedeschia. A kingdom where you have no rights to talk to the King or Prince."

"Zante- what?"

Just then, the guard looked behind me and nodded his head to another guard as though he was signaling the other guards to take me or come closer or even hold me down, worst-case scenario.

"Mortal, you're coming with us..." The other guard dressed in blue, with a muscular build-up, stalked toward me.

I jumped back. "No."

"What did you just say?"

"NO." I stood my ground. I thought of following them inside the castle, up until they said I had no rights to communicate with the Prince.

"Take her."

I was grabbed, and no amount of moving back or squirming had stopped them. As I didn't cooperate by shaking, squirming, and trying to run away, the next moment, the guard grabbed my pepper spray from me and used it against me. He sprayed the damn thing right in my eyes! But I closed them before he did so, anticipating the warning signs. I then screamed for help, but apparently, no one was nearby who could help me. After all, I was in a forest. I didn't particularly feel anyone hit me or even touch me for that matter, but regardless, I blacked out. Darkness took over me.

The next moment, I woke up slowly. I had completely forgotten where I was and what I was doing. I winced and groaned as I felt a stinging in my eyes. I tried to use my fingers to rub my eyes, but as I attempted to do that, I realized my hands were tied. Seriously? Cut me some slack, guys! I heard a noise from behind me, presumably footsteps. I started trembling in fear, and that was when my head was pushed down and dunked into a large basin of cold, cold water.

I screamed, but all that could be heard was my muffled voice. I didn't stop. Somebody yanked my head from the water, and I was still screaming. Now, besides there being a stinging sensation in my eyes because of the pepper spray, I also felt water go down my trachea. I coughed, excessively, I might add.

When the people who had bound me realized that I needed my hands to practically survive, they untied my hands from the chair, from behind me.

I immediately used my hands to rub my eyes, and I could finally feel the stinging sensation lessen (surprisingly). I coughed some more and spit out excess water from my mouth. I opened my eyes. It burned and stung, but I opened them anyway. I wasn't going to die without knowing who to haunt after my death.

I saw three guards surrounding me and the chair I was sitting in, and a young man in a dark coat and tunic standing opposite me.

I immediately eyed his attire up and down, not seeing such clothes still being worn by my generation. I also saw a crown on his head, and I knew he must have been the Prince. I yelled at him, "Please! You must let me go! I didn't do anything!"

"You have no idea what you've started for us. If you, a mortal, found Zantedeschia through our invisible walls sealed in Sugar Hill, then it's a breach and a possibility for more mortals to get in! You're to be punished. This deed will not go unnoticed. Our people are at risk because of you, you're to suffer and die."

"Well, if that's the case and you're not offering me a **chance** to speak and then to proceed to do whatever you want..."

"I'm not."

*He cut me off!* I thought to myself.

"Then **screw you**!" I kicked him in the shin.

He punched my face, and I blacked out. *Again, really? Give a girl a break!*

The next time I woke up, I was lying on a cold, dirty floor and I was inside what looked like a Victorian, abandoned prison. A dungeon.

I screamed for help. A guard came to my aid, or so I thought, until he said, "Pipe down! We don't want to have to knock you out again; this time it'll be more painful."

"How long have I been out of it?" I asked, eyeing him curiously.

"3 hours."

"Oh, hell," I muttered under my breath.

"Hell ain't the worst of it."

"What do you mean?"

"The prince has ordered your execution."

I stopped him.

"Execution? He wants to kill me now?" I said, calmly.

"He always wanted to kill you, child."

"Why do you think I'm a child? I'm almost as old as your dear Prince. How old is he?"

"18."

"17," I replied back. "My age."

He didn't say anything, but he did look surprised. I was now surprised. Back at Sugar Hill, everyone thought I looked too old for my age because of my height. Here, however, everyone thought I looked young for my age.

*What kind of sorcery is this?*

I decided to knock out the guard. And trust me, I can do anything I put my mind to. So, I called him closer to the bars of the prison and then pulled on his collar and pushed him back and forth, again, repeating that for a couple of times until I was sure there was a dent in his brain from all the bashing against the iron bars.

He fell before I could do much damage.

*Yes!* I thought to myself.

Now to get out...

I felt something cold against my ankle, and when I pulled up my bell-bottom jeans, I found a very intricate knife in my sock. It had designs and gemstones all over the handle, and the blade was squeaky clean and as sharp as Sleeping Beauty's spindle on the wheel.

I used it to try and cut the bars of the prison - dungeon - whatever. Dumb idea, I know, cutting thick metal with metal. But I did what I had to do at the time. When I brought the knife closer, though, something extraordinary happened. The knife melted, yes, MELTED, the bars. Liquid iron fell to the floor. I used it to my advantage and melted all the bars before trying to make sense of everything going on.

I ran.

I saw a staircase leading to sunlight, and I ran up the staircase and sprinted toward the setting sun behind the forest.

This was going to lead to the end of me, but I did it anyway.

This was the end. The end of my suffering and the beginning of something incredible. Incredible is an understatement, actually.

Here we go.

*Freya, RUN. And don't look back, I tell myself.*

CHAPTER 3

# Meeting Christopher

I kept running until I was sure I wasn't being seen or followed. That being said, I had to run for quite a while. I tried to hide as I was running, ducking here and there to fit in with the short shrubs and pulling the hoodie over my hair. I ran until I could feel the stone ground transition into something more glassy, the wet soil of the forest. The slippery earth tried to get the best of me, but I didn't allow it. I slipped a couple of times, but I persevered, with a couple of bruises, of course. The rocks underneath my feet scratched the heck out of my skin when I fell. I was out of breath by the time I reached the middle of the forest. I didn't know if I should've gone any further; that was when I remembered the blood-curdling sound I heard the last time I was in this situation before I got caught. And I drew to a halt as the memory rushed back to my brain. What was I supposed to do? I hid behind a tree and started tending to my wounds, which, at this point, started burning, itching, and stinging. Yeah. But I mean, it could be worse. After checking to make sure that my skin wasn't terribly bruised or wounded, I looked ahead of the forest, trying to find out if I could see any town or village where I could seek help. After all, I had no idea where I was.

Zantedeschia, I know. But where **am I?**

I've never heard of a place called Zantedeschia before, and this was apparently a kingdom? *What does that even— never mind. Let's just get the hell out of here and find somebody who can help us.*

I couldn't see further from the trees. The canopy covered everything. I needed to know if there was proof of people on the other side of the forest. I wasn't sure how to figure that out by using a quick technique. Well, there was one way... I quickly decided that I would do it and started removing my shoes. I climbed the trunk of the tree, using my feet to guide me. I reached the canopy after struggling for a couple of minutes, and I tried to see ahead of me. I succeeded. But sadly, all my effort didn't pay off. There was nothing for miles; the forest really did extend over a large portion of the earth. Okay, then, plan B. I slipped and slid down the tree and then decided the only way to get through is by getting to the other side of the 'kingdom.'

The forest was in front of the castle, so I decided to go behind it.

I started to walk, but just as I did so, my arm was pulled back, and I shrieked, only to have my mouth covered by somebody's hand. I was thumped against the back of the tree I had just tried to climb. I screamed, but it was muffled.

"Shh, calm down. I'm not here to hurt you!" the curious-looking boy said. He looked around my age and had especially bright blond hair, more snowy white than blond. I'm sure I could see him from a far distance ahead just because of his hair. His hair was short, and he was wearing a mask, one that looked like it was meant for a masquerade ball. It was black, glossy, and glittery.

He slowly removed his hand from my lips and nodded at me before doing so, as a confirmation that I wouldn't scream again.

I whisper-screamed, "Who... who are you?" and pushed him away.

"Christopher, Prince of Viridesca."

"Prince!" I exclaimed, then tried to run away from him, knowing one thing and making assumptions based on the prince I had just encountered before him.

He caught my arm before twirling me back to him.

"Okay, no. I'm not that type of prince. The prince you probably just encountered is the dark prince of ravens, Corvidus. I'm not him. In fact, I'm nothing like him. I'm from a good kingdom, a good history, and a friendly, if not perfect, personality of people. You can trust me. After all, I'm the one who sent you the knife to help you."

"The knife? The knife!" I quickly realized.

"YES, the knife."

"Okay, talk. You have 5 minutes." I wasn't about to give up my precious time to somebody I hardly even knew.

"I sent you the knife because I had a vision. I can tell when mortals are in trouble from him, Corvidus, especially if they are in trouble in The Magical Realm. It's a skill and talent that took me years to master. I saw you, bruised and thrown into the dungeon. And something in me, I'm not sure what, told me you were innocent and didn't even enter Zantedeschia consciously or on purpose. I had to help; I couldn't see more lives suffer, not when I could do something about it," he sighed.

"What's that supposed to mean?" I asked, eyeing him curiously.

The prince took a deep breath before replying with, "Nothing. Just come on, let's get out of here and talk in a place that's... safer. Can I take you to Emeralda? It's a city within the kingdom I rule, Viridesca. It's where my home is."

"Umm.. I really need to get back..." I told him, with a hint of suspicion in my voice.

"Okay, okay, just 10 minutes, please."

With a lot of hesitation, I told him, "Okay. But I have questions."

"By all means, go ahead."

"Magic. It's real?"

"It always has been."

"I'm going to need more detail than that."

"Yes, magic is real, there are kingdoms here. There are two main kingdoms, surrounding which there are smaller islands. Zantedeschia, and Viridesca. There are other creatures that exist. Vampires, Fae, Centaurs, Griffins, etc. We have somehow managed to remain hidden from the human world through magical barriers sealed and protected by the gods. That's why we are located in a small town like Sugar Hill."

"Ok—"

"Now it's my turn to ask the questions. How'd you find us? Let me guess, science finally got its way?"

"No. Actually, I was transported here automatically."

"Something must have triggered that. Any idea?"

"Hmm, maybe the wildflower I touched at the flea market. It's called — Dames-Violet I think... that's when the visions started."

He grabbed my hand before telling me to close my eyes. I did as he said, I had no idea where this sudden guttural feeling of trust came from, but it did, so I just went ahead with it.

The next moment, I was told to open my eyes, and I saw the same emerald forest I saw last time when I was in the flea market. I was scared, but I tried not to make any rash decisions by screaming. I didn't want to alert unnecessary people.

"This... is Emeralda, Viridesca," the prince, Christopher, told me.

When we landed, I gagged at the floor and threw up. Whatever I had eaten earlier came rushing up, out of my body.

"Whoa, easy."

He held my hair back as I continued retching my guts out at the edge of a tree's stump.

"It takes time to... get used to teleporting. It's not easy, especially for mortals."

He then jumped back in surprise. "You, you're glowing, purple!"

"What?" I asked in confusion.

He said, "Your body is glowing in an outline of neon purple!"

Within seconds, he came closer and said, "it's gone. The glow."

But something absolutely mystical happened next, my hair.

Three strands of my hair turned purple. Three random locks.

They glowed after which they permanently settled on the dark, bright color.

Not only did I witness it, but Christopher did too.

"WHOA!" I stepped back in surprise, holding my long, onyx hair in my hands.

"What the hell?" He came closer and held my hair. There was something sweet and soft about his touch, which immediately made me feel comfortable within his hands.

I quickly pulled back and said, "Okay, I really need to leave now!"

"No. You can't."

My eyes' slits narrowed.

"What did you just say?"

"I'm sorry, you can't leave."

"Wh-why?"

"You could be a magical half breed."

"H-how?!"

"I don't think mortals glow purple, also a name might be nice, I mean I don't want to keep having to not call you by your actual name."

"Freya."

"Freya? You could potentially be half Fae. You need to come with me. We need to do a physical exam on you."

"NO ONE IS TOUCHING ME!" I yelled back in restraint.

"Okay, okay,..." Christopher came closer, I think he was going to hug me to calm me down but he quickly backed away, so I guess we'll never know.

"I- I'm sorry, this is just too much for me! I mean, I don't want to go back to my house where my parents can threaten me and scold me again. I also don't want to be here, but I don't know where else to go!"

"Okay, how's this? Just come with me, I can make you feel comfortable. My palace has many guest rooms, you can stay in one for the night. Just for tonight, if that puts you at more ease, or more nights, if you want."

"Keep talking.."

"I'll give you my protection, in exchange for a physical exam to be done on you."

"Now?"

"No. Umm... tomorrow. Morning. After breakfast."

"Umm. Okay? But how can I be promised my safety from Corv-whatever, with just your word?"

"I'll tell my men to get on it. They guard the Palace anyway; they can guard your room too. I have enough ... resources... just trust me."

"How can I? I don't even know you!"

He came closer and grabbed my palms. I immediately felt a wave of comfort flood over my body. I felt as though I knew I could trust him, It was a gut feeling.

And... I... just knew.

I shrugged off the weird feeling enveloping me.

I was so confused at this point. I mean, there was no way in hell that if I returned to my house now, my parents would let me sleep peacefully for the rest of my life. There's also no way, absolutely NO WAY that I'm half- what was it- Fae? I thought this shit didn't exist. So, I took up the opportunity and questioned him, Prince Christopher.

He led me to a horse that was tied to a tree, and I immediately asked him, "If you could teleport me here then why can't we teleport to your castle?"

"It doesn't work that way. Magic can only be used for teleporting in emergency situations. It's not easy to use that type of magic and it takes a lot of energy out of the person using that magic. Unless you want me to faint by the time we reach the castle, it's better we go there by horse."

"But... I'm sort of scared..."

He let out a low chuckle.

"Of me? Or the horse?"

I smiled at the joke and told him "The horse. I've never ridden before."

"Really?"

"Yes. I'm, not so good with animals."

"Really? Well, go figure." He laughed again.

"It's not scary at all, just shaky, a little more than you'd expect from a horse this size. And of course, it depends on the speed. We must travel fast now because it's getting late, and the Fleskies might come after you. After all, we don't even know if you're human or Fae. Or half human, half Fae." His hand reached out in my direction.

I took it and, somehow, magically, managed to climb the horse without fear and with help.

I felt better now, from all my throwing up and bruises.

I breathed deeply as he climbed in front of me, and we started riding our way to the castle.

My hair flew back in the wind, and I felt like a warrior princess on her way back to her castle, but I didn't say anything, the thought made me feel childish and embarrassed all on its own.

I told the prince, "Can we stop for a minute, I need to tie my hair, I'm really sweaty, I think it's all the teleporting and anxiety of the situation we're in."

"Sure, you okay though?"

"I guess, I'll be clearer when we stop."

He slowed down and pulled the horse back. "Easy boy, easy Marcus."

I grinned and then asked, "His name is Marcus? Cute."

"Don't say that to his face, he'll eat you up and spit you out."

I threw my head back and laughed.

We eventually stopped, and I tied my hair into a plait. It felt easier to handle all that weight when it was tied up, and I never had the heart to cut it. I noticed the purple locks as I did so. I tried smudging it out on my hand, nothing happened, I don't know what I was expecting.

Christopher smiled and said, "it's not dyed with chalk for you to smudge it against your palm. It's probably not going to be washed out either, although you can sure try."

"I know, I don't know what I was thinking."

I paused before telling him that I was ready to go again, and we picked up pace.

"I have a lot of questions."

"As a mortal, I'm sure you do."

"Can you stop saying that? I'm not some useless species. You can address me by my name."

"You can call me Christopher, or Chris, you know, whatever suits you."

"Why? Aren't I a lower class than you? Shouldn't I be addressing you as 'My Lord'?"

"I don't think it's necessary, besides, I don't feel that way." A corner of his lips lifted, as though he was smiling at me, in his own mysterious way.

## Chapter 4

# Mortal (Not)

We reached the castle in fair time, and Christopher guided me to my (guest) room for the time being. He left me, of course, after asking me if I wanted or needed anything, to which I asked him for a meal and a glass of water. The Prince guided me to the royal dining room, which was quite close to the foyer on the first floor of the colossal castle.

He let me sit where I wanted, and after fidgeting for a bit, unsure as to how to ask him, I ended up saying that my place of comfort, which was my room, was where I wanted to be. I really felt the need for privacy, after everything that had happened, I was still tingly with the... what's the word? Angst? Apprehension? Disquietude?

I ate my spaghetti in silence, the only noises that I could hear were the soft chewing of the spaghetti strands, heavy breathing and the chirping of crickets and cicadas from the evergreen trees outside the window which was open.

After finishing my dinner, which I ate without shame as my body filled with the satisfaction of my hunger being tamed, I took a deep breath and fell to the bed. Within minutes, I got into such a deep sleep that I started dreaming.

That was that for the night.

I woke up the next morning to a maid? Yes, a maid, I guess, who was knocking on my door and entered after I asked her to come in politely. She said breakfast was ready and that was when I asked her to tell me the time, to which she responded saying "10am". I jumped.

I realized that I overslept, probably for the best, I did need energy to hear what I assumed I was going to hear after the results of the physical exam came out.

I was actually glad that I slept peacefully. It had been a while since that happened.

"Okay. Thank you, for informing me about breakfast, I'll be there in twenty. Can I also please have some toiletries and a towel?"

"It's already in the bathroom miss."

"Thanks again." I closed the door behind the maid and rushed into the bathroom to take a quick shower and brush my teeth.

I allowed the hot water to scald my skin as I tried to figure out the temperature and pressure settings of the showerhead and came out after 30 minutes and combed through my hair. I got ready, wearing the same clothes as yesterday as I was somewhat persistent to ask for a change of clothes. I felt it might've been disrespectful to demand so many things all at once. I applied some strawberry scented lip gloss and scrambled downstairs to the dining room.

I stopped short after seeing Christopher leaning against the wall, staring at me by the table filled and splayed neatly with breakfast breads, pastries, pancakes, waffles, and eggs.

I took a deep breath; I never noticed his beauty up until now.

"Morning." He said.

"Good morning." I replied.

"Have a seat, won't you?"

I sat down as far away from him as possible, considering the rush of adrenaline that went through my body as I just saw him. I thought it was for the best.

"I'm sorry I took so long to get ready.."

"No, don't apologize. You didn't change your clothes?"

"No, but I took a shower. I promise." My cheeks turned pink.

He chuckled before saying, "I believe you... Miss Annette will give you some new clothes which should be appropriate and comfortable for you, I think I may have your style figured out. You're one of those girls who prefer comfort over fashion, aren't you?"

I didn't reply, my cheeks turning red next.

"Thank you.."

"No problem... aren't you going to eat?"

"Aren't you?"

"I already did."

"Oh, I see."

"I hope you're not offended that I didn't wait for you?"

"No, not at all!"

"Good. I was hungry, so..."

There was then a moment of awkward silence.

"Yeah, okay.... So..."

"So?"

"So..."

I tried to frame words in my mind as I picked up a croissant.

"Are you ready for the physical exam to happen after breakfast? We have a qualified doctor here now.."

"Sure, I'm ready..."

"Alright."

Christopher waited as I finished eating up whatever was left.

After breakfast, the Prince extended his hand, I took it and felt the warmth of his palm embody me.

He guided me outside the palace, to a small tent located just at the back. I entered with him, only to see what appeared to be a female doctor ready to do my physical.

She asked me some basic questions about my life.

My family, my lineage, my age, my blood type, etc.

She then examined my hands as Chris told her about how I glowed purple yesterday.

She took one look at them and said"Mmm, interesting."

She then saw my hair, specifically the locks that turned purple.

She then took some notes in her writing pad and said,

"You.. you're quite interesting."

"How so?" Christopher spoke before I had a chance to.

"She, she's definitely no mortal..."

I dropped onto the table, in utter shock.

"C-" Chris started speaking, but I cut him off.

"Could the test results be wrong by any chance?" I asked.

"Nope," she replied quickly.

"Is she Fae?" The prince asked.

"No. Well, we couldn't, we wouldn't know until she can consciously see and use her powers."

"So.. she's a changeling?.."

"Yes, I'm sure of it," the examiner told him.

"Thank yo—"

"What does that mean?" I asked, my impatience and curiosity getting the best of me.

"It means—" The examiner started talking, but Christopher cut her off.

"It means, Freya, that you were created in another woman's womb, and then you were magically transferred to Sugar Hill's hospital when you were born. This says that your parents adopted you, and well, never told you about it."

I was stunned. My eyes started pooling with water, and my mouth started twitching.

I ran back inside the castle, clearly not prepared for the answer I got.

I kept running until I reached my guest room. I slammed the door shut and bawled my eyes out. What the hell was going on? How was this even remotely possible? Is there a chance that all of this is not true?

I doubted it. Even though I felt I was in denial, something in me knew that the examiner was **not** lying to me. Especially, not to Chris: **THE PRINCE's face.**

Something was off... something was not right...

I walked back and forth across my room. Back and forth and back and forth... biting my nails and running my hand through my hair. Rummaging through the change of clothes I had and screaming from internal pain. My scream echoed through the halls of the castle. I heard footsteps, and when I looked toward the door of my room, I saw Christopher running in. He grabbed my arms and hugged me, tight.

"I'm sorry.."

"It's not your fault..." I said, crying into his shoulder.

"We can find your real parents... I won't stop until I do.."

"What's it to you? You barely know me..." I sobbed into his chest, breathing heavily, almost having a panic attack...

"You've had a lasting impression on me since I first saw you in my vision. I will help you, trust me..."

"I- I do."

Chris spent the next hour hugging and trying to calm me down. But I couldn't bear the pain... I was adopted...

and I didn't know why my real parents gave me up. The single thought that hurt me the most was the thought of them giving me up because they didn't want me rather than anything else being the reason.

After some time, Christopher left me alone to wallow in some privacy, and I did exactly that.

What was sweet of him, though, was the fact that he sent me some flowers, roses, and chocolates up to my room at midnight through Miss Annette.

I tried to sleep, I really did, but I just couldn't, well, everything considered.

My face looked puffy, and my eyes were red the next morning.

I was still wallowing; I didn't want to shower, eat, or do anything else. I wasn't in the mood for any of it.

At 8 am, Christopher knocked on my door and came in after I told him to.

I sat upright on the bed and looked at him sternly.

"Listen, I would really appreciate if you allowed me to stay here in Emeralda for a couple more days, maybe weeks, until I find out about my history and family. I understand not being allowed to stay in the castle; I also need my own privacy. If you could just help me find a job where I could earn money to rent a place, then I would really be grateful to you."

Chris started to speak, but I cut him off.

"It's just something I… I need to do."

"I understand."

I tried to smile, but it didn't appear on my face.

Christopher resumed talking, "That's why…"

He lifted his hand and showed me a key with a couple of pink keychains on them.

"I'm sorry, I picked out the keychains, and I don't know what color girls like." He grinned.

"Girls like pink, generally, … but I'm not like other girls," I smiled and told him.

"What's this for anyway? A car? If so, I really can't accept—"

"It's for your new (temporary) home. A cabin, in the woods, not too far from the castle."

My eyes opened wide, and my jaw dropped to the floor.

"W-what do you mean?"

"A cabin. For you to stay in. After all, every non-mortal deserves her own privacy! Oh, also, here you go, a red-buttoned pager, use it for emergencies to call me."

I hugged him. "Thank you."

He nodded in acceptance.

"You'll find a couple of new clothes, some toiletries, and everything else a girl like you needs for a couple of days, or weeks.. so don't bother asking Miss Annette for anything else unless you actually need anything else."

"Done. Thanks again, Chris..."

"Wow."

"What?"

"I think that's the first sign you're seeing me as more than just a savior of a damsel in distress and as a Prince.."

I grinned.

The next couple of days went by quite peacefully.

I got settled into my new cabin and felt a mix of emotions. I didn't know how to react for a while, but then I realized that I couldn't do anything about the current situation except accept it as it was.

So that's what I did.

After 2 days of settling in, Christopher and I were talking, and he said he wanted to introduce me to the court of the kingdom and show me around. He thought it might get my mind off of things.

I happily accepted his offer.

We started off by first having a court dance where I could be introduced to the court members as a new addition to the kingdom's population of Fae. (We all assumed I would be Fae since it's practically impossible to be considered as any other creature; it's just not possible for a changeling. The more complex the creature, the harder it is to put that baby in the mortal world.)

Skipping ahead to the night before the court dance, I was given a special gown by Chris, sent through Miss Annette. I smiled when I received the gift, happily changing into it the next day.

It was a mixture of greens, purples, and turquoise, filled with intricate designs and gemstones glued onto the upper half of the dress. It looked... magnificent.

I wasn't dressed for riding, but I craved a horse ride one more time before the dance, and so I rode my horse (which was given to me by Christopher to keep at the stable outside my cabin) all the way back to the castle.

It was fun, but I had horse hair all over my dress; good thing I carried a lint roller with me.

I smoothed out my dress and left to go inside the castle, leaving my horse at the royal stables. I named her Izzy.

I entered the castle's ballroom through the grand staircase. I started walking down as heads turned and the frequency of whispers increased. I started noticing the room. The dance floor was a large open space, made of marble. There were elevated balconies overlooking the dance floor with some seats.

There was a group of people playing music on the stage, which was a small, elevated platform.

There was also a small parlor adjacent to the musicians' area, which I assumed was for private conversations.

I saw a large chandelier overhead, gleaming, as I could smell the smoky incense of burning candles.

I could also hear the rustle of gowns as people were walking around and dancing.

I walked slowly, trying not to trip over the length of my own dress.

Chris appeared and extended an arm as I reached the floor level.

I took his arm in mine and locked our hands together.

I was introduced to the people of the court of Viridesca.

"Hello, love, you must be Ms. Nyx. Freya, was it?" A tall man started speaking, to which I replied with, "You got that right..."

"Are you sure you're Fae?" His hand reached behind my ears, trying to push my hair back. I felt extremely uncomfortable, and apparently, I displayed the feeling of discomfort too.

"You don't need to flinch, love; I'm just checking to see if you have pointed ears.."

"Pointed ears? Why? And no, I'm not sure if I'm Fae yet."

"You don't know, do you? All Fae have pointed ears."

"I thought that was for Elves."

He and the court laughed.

"Love, not everything you read out of fairytale books is true..."

"Oh.."

"Yes, 'oh.'"

He chugged down a shot of what looked like whiskey.

"I didn't get your name.."

"Felix."

Chris walked up to us and managed to make me feel more comfortable throughout the rest of the conversation.

The rest of the night sped by, and I felt mystical and magical in such a scenery. It was quite nice, was it not for the uncomfortable conversations held by the court members.

Whatever, let's just call it a day is what I thought.

The next day, Chris had a long conversation with me talking about the powers of Fae and what they can do.

Apparently, all Fae had magical powers.

They could use the powers of the four elements: air, fire, water, and earth to bend magic to their will.

It depended and differed from different classes of Fae. This was the case in Zantedeschia, but here, in Viridesca, all Fae were treated equally and could all have and maintain the same powers.

It seemed amazing. I was still in shock and awe of the fact that such a place even existed. It was just... what's the word? Otherworldly.

## Chapter 5

# Fleski

A week went by with careful monitoring of my powers. No powers had developed yet. Everyone, including the court, had become wary of me. I was starting to get worried. Well, that's an understatement.

I was really freaking concerned.

There was then a good chance I wasn't even Fae, which started many rumors throughout the court and the majority of the kingdom.

A week later, on a Tuesday morning, there was a court meeting in order. Christopher told me that they would be discussing me and the chances that I'm still human, or at least not Fae. Whatever that meant.

Okay, so, this is what it had come to.

Fine. Manageable. I guess.

I just had to make a good enough impression so that the court didn't throw me out onto the streets or into some other dungeon.

Even the prince can't do anything about that. The court's decision is always final. Weird. It doesn't work that way back at 'home'.

So, I decided to do what I could do best. Woo the audience.

The meeting happened in an hour. Best to use that time wisely.

So I got ready, quickly putting on a tunic and pants that looked decent enough and were also oddly comfortable. I waited, biting my nails, walking back and forth across my cabin, and just plainly staring out into the wilderness through my window.

The court meeting started, and unlike my first impression toward the court, I did NOT make a grand entrance. It seemed unnecessary, obviously.

The discussions started shortly after we all got settled in.

The first member of the court stated, "Miss Freya's powers have not yet developed. There could be many reasons for this, so let's not rush into a deep-headed argument just yet.

First of all, let's talk to the girl, after all, she's here, and she definitely must have something to say. Miss Freya?"

I stiffened at the call of my name. My slightly arched back bent up straight.

"Umm... I can attest to the fact that none of my so-called powers have yet developed.

It's true that I may not be Fae, maybe just human. Actually, that makes more sense to me than of the fact that I'm Fae. So, my suggestion? We wait it out, a little longer."

"My dear, sweet girl, as much as you may be right, we cannot allow you to simply stay here without proof that you deserve to live in Viridesca. It needs to be earned. And if, after all, you are human, we will have to send you back after erasing your memory of this place. It's just not fair, letting you stay here, you see?"

"I understand, sir. However, I discovered this place without the proper operation and guidance of my prefrontal cortex and hippocampus, the parts of the brain related to decision making. After all, I didn't really get a say in coming here, did I? It makes more sense to me that I should be allowed to stay here since I'm causing no harm to you and your people and only want accommodation. You hear?"

"This girl and her nerve." Another man said to the first member of the court. I smirked.

This girl and her nerve, alright. Loser.

I spoke again... "Have none of you considered the fact that I could be more of a threat rather than a liability? You're not sure I'm Fae, and I'm not sure either. But how can you be so sure that I'm nothing worse?"

That was the moment I realized I dug my own grave, real, real deep.

"You are right, dear." The first member spoke with confidence.

"You could very well pose as a threat." He spoke sarcastically, the sarcasm simmered for a bit and only settled after the entire court started laughing, tilting all their heads back.

"I was serious." I cleared my throat.

"Oh, very well. What do you suppose you could be? Any images in your head popping in randomly? Any weird, recurring thoughts, numbers, or dreams you notice?"

"No such thing so far." I stared ahead into the crowd.

That was when I started hearing whispers between the members of the court.

"She could be Fleski?" Felix, one of the court members I met earlier at the ball, mentioned.

I was stunned. Taken aback. *Did he really just call me.. that.. thing?*

"Right now, you're staying at a cabin in the woods offered to you by our young man, the Prince, am I right?"

"Yes." I answered plainly.

Some more whispering went down. I could see eyebrows rise and people show expressions of shock for at least 10 minutes before I was spoken to again.

"You might need to stay in a cell or a guarded room, where we have a lot of our guards looking after your behavior."

"What the hell is that supposed to mean?" I spat back in anger, a hand moving to be placed on my hip.

"It means... you could genuinely be a threat."

"So why protect me? Why not kill me now?"

"Dear, we aren't protecting you... we're observing you and your actions. You say you haven't seen any powers develop as of yet, but how should we trust you?"

"Because!" I didn't have any words to say.

"Because?"

Silence.

"That's what I thought."

I can't believe I didn't have a good comeback, but it made sense. I was put on the spot.

After a lot of discussing and maneuvering by Chris, the court decided that I could stay at the cabin for a while more. A week, maybe two. Our side won! I was given some more time to access my powers and figure out what the hell I was. By the skies! That was relieving to hear.

I realized one thing though... I had to tap into my powers sooner rather than later if I was allowed to stay here.

Sometime after the court meeting, I decided to head back into my cabin. I felt exhausted and needed some sleep desperately.

As soon as I reached the place, I kicked off my shoes, which were coated with moist and damp mud from the woods, and I curled up with a book that was in my own personal, mini-library that Christopher prepared for me to be busy in my cabin. I only had the reading lamp's light on.

But soon enough, just as I was about to flip one of the pages of my book, I heard a noise.

The reading lamp started to blink vigorously, and my kitchen tap started running water. I stopped reading and switched on the main lights. They started flickering and blinking as well.

On, off. On, off. On off.

I was starting to get worried. I tried to listen carefully, trying to figure out what was going on. And that was when I heard what seemed like chittering, once more. It was very similar to the first sound that I heard.

I figured the noise was coming from outside the cabin, originating in the woods. I waited once more, trying to figure out whether it was all my imagination or the noises were real.

They were real.

I quickly pulled my hair into a ponytail and started looking around the cabin for any weapons. I found some knives in the kitchen and an ax, which was probably here for chopping down wood to make a fire.

I grabbed whatever I could and positioned myself next to the window, continuing to pace back and forth before I locked the door and pushed a table against it so nobody (or should I say nothing) could enter.

Just then, my memory came rushing into my mind, reminding me to use the pager to call Christopher if anything went wrong.

I foolishly waited, though, thinking there was no such threat that involved me calling the Prince of the kingdom immediately. I would discuss this with him tomorrow.

My window broke. The glass shards scratched my cheek and neck, and I tried looking outside while choking back my tears. I was really frightened. Could it just be a wild animal? Or something way worse?

Just then, as I was trying to analyze my thoughts, a large spider-like human being with black ooze dripping from its body and a weight and size that looked like nothing I'd ever seen before crashed into my cabin through the window.

I screamed and backed away, pointing my ax and knife toward it.

It circled me, eyeing me with curiosity, as though it had never seen a person like me before. And yet, it completely invaded my personal space. Not that that was important during such a time of crisis. I tried reaching the pager button behind it, but it blocked the way, so I quickly took my ax and sliced its head right across the neck before I grabbed the pager button and quickly, yet silently, pushed it hard.

The pager started beeping and blinking red lights. Maybe he was on his way. Christopher.

I backed away again, trying to find new ways to survive as I realized that the creature grew two more heads in the place where I sliced its first head off. I was stunned, utterly in shock. I ran outside only to find more of the same type of creatures surrounding my cabin, and I screamed yet again while trying to think my way out of this mess. Fear overtook me, and I didn't know what to do or how to proceed.

The castle was not nearly close enough. Just as I was planning my next steps, I realized I took too long to decide because that was when I felt a large spike enter my stomach from the side, and I yelped before I could say much.

The spike went through my entire body, and I felt paralyzed from the waist down as what felt like an oozy liquid burst through my body. Venom, I assumed. I fell to the ground with a thud. Just then I heard somebody screaming my name. A voice that sounded a little too much like Christopher. "Freya! Freya! Where are you? Freya, are you okay?" He screamed my name.

I also heard multiple footsteps which I assumed were the guards who realized I had been attacked.

My vision was blurry when I looked up, and saw a fuzzy image of someone lifting me up and hooking an arm around my shoulder and neck to help me walk. That was when I fell to the floor again, not being able to feel my legs, and blacked out within mere seconds.

The next moment that I awoke, my sight was blurry and I was chilly. I could smell the scent of rubbing alcohol and hand sanitizer. I was curious. Where was I?

"Freya? Are you okay? Freya?" Someone, most likely Christopher, asked me. I couldn't see him clearly, but I knew he was there.

"Christopher? I'm afraid... wait, what happened?"

I asked him, trembling with fear. I felt a sharp pain throbbing in my side.

Slowly my vision became clearer. I was suddenly able to remember what happened. The Fleski- they came after me. They hurt me.

"Chris? Thank you... thank you for... saving me..." I silently whispered to him. My eyes were still processing my surroundings. I reached out to hug him, and as I did, I winced in pain from pulling at my side. He hugged me back.

"You're okay... You're okay, Freya."

I started to whimper and cry. I knew that I would be alright, but the whole experience put me into shock.

I breathed deeply, in and out, in and out.

I started to look around; it looked like I was in a medical room, and I was wearing a surgical gown. A blanket was put over me.

"Wh-where am I?"

"In the medical room back at the castle... you had to undergo stitches where the Fleski got you."

"Why were they after me? What-what did I do?"

A pause. Silence.

"That's the thing, Freya, you didn't do anything, right? I mean, I'm sure you didn't attack or trigger them?

Generally speaking, Fleskies don't go after Fae. We have an agreement. We have taken great precautions to ensure they do not harm Fae, and, well, me and the Court, we're sure it wouldn't have come after you unless you were perceived as a threat to them... Now there's an even better chance that you may not be Fae."

I gasped.

"What?"

"I'm only telling you the truth."

"The- then... what am I?"

"We- we don't know.. besides, your powers haven't even been developed yet so that doesn't help us too..."

I sighed before settling down in the medical room bed again.

"Couldn't you guys have used magic to fix me up? Were stitches really necessary?"

"Magic doesn't work like that. And we did use magic to remove the venom."

"Oh, sorry, I don't mean to come off as... I can't seem to find the right word."

He stroked my hair back, "You don't need to right now. Just rest..."

"I suggest you continue to stay in the castle henceforth. It's risky to stay out alone in the woods with these Fleski after you."

"So, back to the castle, huh?"

"Yep."

"I'm not Fae?"

"Most likely not."

# Chapter 6

# Freya's House

Three days went by in impatience and pain, pain from my wounds and impatience from waiting for my powers to develop. It really takes forever, doesn't it? I decided on something, maybe not the best decision but good enough for the moment. I wanted to go back to my home (house, really...) and talk to my so-called parents about my adoption. Chances are they weren't going to speak to me about anything, forget my adoption, but I wouldn't give up without a fight.

So the next step would be to ask Christopher what he thought and what he suggested. This may not be the best decision, and I was well aware of that. But I wasn't giving up. Wait, I already said that. *Why am I in denial already? Repeating sentences to yourself - not good, Freya. It is a sign of weakness, and I'm not here for that.* Clearly, I was procrastinating more and more. No point in that. I finally decided to go and talk to Christopher. I needed him to let me go, finally allow me out of the castle regardless of the risks relating to the Fleskies.

***

"Are you bullshitting me right now?" Christopher queried, in annoyance.

"I'm being serious, Chris." I replied, cringing in pain from my stomach wounds still healing.

"Well, that sounds more like a joke, Freya!"

"Come on, I need to go back!"

"Why? Why do you need to go back so badly? What have they given you that's so important for you to return to? Oh, that's right - nothing!"

"Tell me, why do you want me to stay? I wasn't in your life before all this happened... what makes you ask me to stay back?"

"You- You're..." A pause, he straightened his back before continuing with

"...important to me."

"Why? Is it because I could be an important asset to your kingdom's growth? Because I could possibly be more than Fae? Something better?"

"This is not okay. You can't speak to me like this! I'm the ruler of this kingdom. You cannot disrespect me."

I didn't reply. I just looked down.

"Fine, Freya, do what you want but if Fleskies come after you again I won't be there to save you!" Christopher yelled.

"Whatever, Chris – Y- you don't understand!"

"Then make me understand!"

"I need to know why I was adopted, I need to know who my real parents are, and know what made them think "Let's adopt her!" and then treat me like crap. It just doesn't add up."

There was just silence for the next two minutes. I was starting to feel uncomfortable. And then I started to talk again when Chris just came close to me and hugged me tight.

"I'm concerned, Freya. You need to see this from my point of view..."

"I understand, but I'll do my best to be safe. Trust me, I can handle myself. After all, I've taken care of myself for 17 years."

"Fine. Alright, but it's important that you maintain a low profile at all times. No one, and I mean no one, can know that magic exists. You need to be wary and cautious of unknown threats, Freya. There may be many dangers now that everyone knows you're not Fae. You might be targeted!"

"By whom?"

"By everyone! If anyone sees you as a threat, then you are done for. Everyone is wary of everyone, even as Fae. Imagine how wary they will be if they think that you are not Fae?"

"Alright, alright, I get it. I'll be careful!"

"Okay then."

"Okay." I slowly smiled at him, trying to mentally say "Thank you."

Christopher then proceeded to explain to me how to get back home. Apparently, there's a magical door hidden in the forest of Emeralda. I was supposed to think of where I wanted to be and then walk through the door, which would lead to the destination's closest forest and drop me there. I had to be sure to get there without being caught by any of the Fleskies. Christopher asked me if I needed him or anyone else to accompany me to the magic door, but I told him that this was something I needed to do on my own. So, he let me. Although he told me to be cautious, which, let me guarantee you, I was. He drew me a map of where the exact location of the door was supposed to be.

"So... This is where we say goodbye?"

"I guess."

We stared at each other, trying to communicate through our emotions.

"I – I hope you remember everything I told you…"

"I do."

"I'll see you soon, Freya."

"Bye, Chris."

He slowly walked away from me, back in the direction that we came. I started to head toward the forest of Emeralda by horse. I climbed on top of the new horse and started my journey. It was not too long; I reached the center of the forest within fifteen to twenty minutes. I then tied up my horse to a tree and proceeded to look at the map Chris had drawn me. The door was not too far off from where I was standing. But that was exactly when I started hearing chittering again. So I ran, knowing full well what to expect. *Sorry, dear horse, I didn't mean to get you killed.*

I finally reached the location of the door. I took one look behind me to see black Fleskies appearing, and I ran into the door. I reached Sugar Hill, New Hampshire within seconds that it took me to walk through the door. I shut the door with a lot of effort and left the place.

Hopefully the Fleskies wouldn't enter through the door.

I started to pace toward the direction of my house. It clearly wasn't too far off, just a few minutes by walk, I'd get there faster if I **paced** my way to the house. And even faster, if I **sprinted.**

I got there after ten minutes of walking and sweating. I finally brought up the courage to ring the bell.

But as soon as the door opened, I saw my mom and dad, and... Corvidus! He was holding a dagger to their throats!

***

"You!" I screamed into his face.

"Yes, sweetheart?"

"Let my parents go. Right. Now." I came closer and pushed him back, or at least tried to. But his chest felt like it was made of steel and he wouldn't budge. I cursed under my breath.

"What do you want? By the Skies— What do you want from me?!"

"Relax, I won't harm your parents."

"The dagger you're holding to their throats says otherwise!"

I tried to pull the dagger from his grasp but only ended up with a kick to my stomach. I fell to the floor as I shouted, "Hey! EASY! I just got stitches there!"

"Come with me, and your parents are safe."

"You know what, do whatever the hell you want with them, I don't care about them anyways, they never looked after me, why should I give a shit about them?"

"Oh really?" He smirked, before pushing my dad away forcefully and almost choking my mom.

Corvidus grabbed the knife and started cutting through my mom's neck. He was going slow and steady, regardless, her neck started to bleed. And that was when I decided enough was enough.

"OKAY! Okay! I'll come with you. JUST leave her alone. Leave them alone!"

That was when my mom started talking. "Yes! Take that little rugrat. We don't need her, do whatever you want with her, kill her if need be, just leave us alone!"

He laughed before saying, "It's a done deal."

He pushed them aside before grabbing my hand and now positioning the knife to my throat, almost choking me out the same way he did to my mom.

"Hey! What do you think you're doing?!"

"What? You think I'll go easy on you? After all, I know your tactics for escaping. However, poor Chris won't be here to save you this time."

CHAPTER 7

# Zantedeschia

Corvidus took what I would assume to be a magical powder and blew it into my face. It was iridescent and sparkly, almost like what I assumed to be ground unicorn horn. We immediately were teleported back to Zantedeschia, and I fell face-first onto the floor. "Ow!" I exclaimed.

"What the h-hell?" I looked around to see five people standing around me in a circle. As soon as they saw me, they started chanting something and holding their hands together. Immense pain shot through my body, and I was magically bound to a chair behind me, which I hadn't noticed earlier. It was unbelievable! Invisible strings tied me to the chair and put me in place. I was shocked. Their power, the power of these people, was much stronger than I assumed or realized.

I was then pulled back, and my legs and ankles were tied to the bottom of the chair, and a thick chain was placed around my neck. It was big, strong, and heavy. *Why is all this necessary?* was all that went through my head as I sat through this, breathing heavily.

"So, this is her, I guess," one of the girls surrounding me stated.

"Yeah, why were we expecting more?" another guy said.

"HEY!" I started talking but was cut off by a slap.

"Who do you think you are? We will do as we please with you, at least that's what Prince Corvidus has told us."

"Who are you people?"

"We're the secret circle of Zantedeschia."

"What's that?"

"You don't need to know. Do as we say before you end up getting hurt."

"What do you even want from me?"

"Nothing much, sugarplum, just your secrets, your magic, and well, everything else that you have but have been hiding from the Prince."

I kicked and screamed.

"Let me go!"

"No," she replied condescendingly.

"Oh, Corvidus will want to see this; he is bound to enjoy all of her... reactions," one of the boys proudly stated.

"You think you're so smart, but this isn't the end of it. Christopher will come looking for me, and when he does, you're all screwed."

"Oh, is that so?" The same boy replied condescendingly.

"It is."

"You have no idea who Christopher even is, do you?"

"What do you mean?"

"Well, why spoil all the fun when Corvidus can have you for himself?"

"I promise, this isn't the end of it. You're all dead! You hear me? DEAD!" I swore to them.

"This is just... I thought you magical creatures were kinder than this."

"You ain't seen nothing yet, kid." I could hear Corvidus saying this, but I couldn't see him anywhere around me. *What a creep.*

***

The secret circle left me alone to brood in the darkness. But I knew I was being watched, maybe through some magical means or just plain old technology. Perhaps through cameras? Time floated by carelessly. I kept attempting to escape somehow, kicking my legs, yelling, and trying to figure out where the knot for the invisible bonds and ropes was so I could undo them. It was all difficult strategies, but they had to be attempted.

After what seemed like hours but was probably just an hour, a dark shadow entered the room. I was trembling for two reasons. One was genuinely the temperature of the room; it was freezing. The other was because of the unknown person entering the room, the shadow.

"Who the hell is there?" I hollered.

"Nobody that you don't know..."

"Who. The. Hell. Is. There?"

The person, or perhaps I should say shadow, who was talking to me, came into the light.

I breathed before saying, "Corvidus."

"Freya," he responded.

"How do you know my name?"

Silence was all that was answered.

"How do you know my name!" I repeated.

"I just do. No biggie."

"God, you're so lame; you make me cringe."

"Oh, do I now? Well, at least I've accomplished something in life then."

I didn't reply or respond. I hoped that the elimination of noise would make him realize what a grave mistake he's making.

It didn't, at least not that I know of.

"What do you want? First hurting my parents and then hurting me? **Not cool**, man!"

"It's not that I actually hurt anyone... just yet... so you're wrong there."

"Are you just here to point out all of my mistakes? Or do you have something genuine to say?"

"Maybe," he continued, "You're a bigger, spoiled brat than we all anticipated..."

I got angrier than expected and ended up smiling, just to throw him off.

And let me tell you, that was a bad decision to make.

Whack! A slap to my face. My cheek turned red, I'm sure of it, even though I couldn't see anything at the time.

"What the hell was that for?"

"You were going to get it sometime anyway. Just a matter of sooner or later."

I cursed at him.

A smile, and then, "You really think we're all going to go easy on you, but the secret circle follows whatever I say, and I can make your life a living hell." A smirk.

"**Just** leave me alone. Or kill me, because I'd sure as hell do anything else than spend time with you."

"Trust me, it's not over yet. So, let's sit down, shall we? We need to have a little talk…"

Corvidus started toying around with what looked like torture devices.

I was shaking.

"What did Christopher want with you?"

"Nothing! He wanted to save me!"

"From what?"

"From whom, actually, and from YOU!"

"What did you learn about from Christopher's kingdom, Viridesca?"

"Absolutely nothing! He has nothing to hide!"

"Funny, sweetheart. Answer correctly, and your fingers will remain intact. Capiche?"

"What did they want with you? Christopher and the court?"

"They wanted to help me."

"Help you with what?"

I didn't speak. I knew I said too much already.

He slapped me again.

**"Help you with what!"**

"I can't tell you!"

He started toying around with a knife. At the sight of this, I started quivering.

He came closer. I started shaking in my seat, trying to get the ropes loose so I could run away, but it was no use. He took the knife and held my hair in his hands.

"I know what girls and women treasure... beauty, makeup, their perfect facial features, their long locks."

"Where are you going with this? And, by the way, you have no idea how insanely wrong you are."

He took in a deep breath, then started pulling my head back by tugging on my hair.

"Please, just try and tell me how wrong I am, let's see what happens."

"Hey! **Stop!**"

He started cutting the locks of my hair, with the knife so deep in that it started scraping my neck.

"That hurts!"

"Oh, did I start scraping your neck? That wasn't my intention, believe it or not."

"I don't."

He eventually got through cutting all my hair. All that was left was the shoulder-length locks of my purple-streaked, black hair.

*Psycho. Absolute psychopath.*

**"Leave me alone! I hate you!"**

"Yeah, the feeling's mutual, honey."

"You think you're so smart, but cutting my hair isn't going to make me cry, or holler, or scream. You're only giving me more strength. After all, beauty lies **within**."

"Now look who's cringe?" He laughed.

"How about I start scraping your heart out? Will beauty still lie within? Or better yet, I'll cut through your brain so you'll never be able to talk or remember anything ever again."

Silence.

"Are you ready to talk?"

"NO!" I spat back.

"Okay then."

He opened up a bag and took out what looked like herbs.

"This is Scelena. It's toxic to Fae, but more toxic to mortals. If you don't start talking, I'm going to have to use this."

I couldn't help the fear. I started talking, the truth. "I may be Fae."

"What?"

"There's a chance I'm Fae and not a mortal."

Corvidus smiled, "Thank you."

And chucked the herbs in my face.

They stung, they burned, they burst in my face.

I screeched in pain.

I was ready to plan my revenge. And man, oh man, would it **burn.**

I was left screaming and groaning. By the time Corvidus had returned, he hadn't come alone. The secret circle accompanied him.

***

They strode in like they were the main characters of some movie and went to the corner of the room where the torture devices were.

"So, what'd she say?" One of the members of the secret circle asked Corvidus.

"Maybe Fae."

"Maybe Fae? That's what she said?" Another member yelled.

The rest of them were shaking their heads back and forth in a 'no' motion and were tsking.

"She's lying to you. Can't you see that?" She repeated to him.

"Maybe, but it's hard to tell. If she is lying, she's great at convincing me otherwise."

"Throw that piece of shit where it belongs! And teach her a freaking lesson for lying!"

"No."

"What?"

Silence.

"You're making a grave mistake, your highness."

"I want to hear it from her, the pleads, the sorrys, the cries... I want to hear her, see her suffer."

"Great idea! How about we verbally torture her? Physically torturing her will only result in screams. Verbally abusing her may at least result in some answers."

"Fair point," Corvidus said.

"Let's try it."

They all nodded, including the prince, and came up to me.

"The reason we've discussed what we've discussed here is so that you can hear our plans and prepare accordingly. It's not going to bode well for you, so we've taken pity on you, to endure your last few moments of peace before suffering and pleading for death."

I smiled, then laughed.

"Do you even know me? I have insane willpower, you **can't** break me, and I will make sure that for every second that you torture me, I will never cry. That should teach you."

"Just because you had the nerve to say that, I'm going to make sure you cry. I'll make sure you suffer and whimper until you promise me you'll keep crying out loud. It's NOT a game, Freya," Corvidus promised me as he stalked closer to the chair, his words laced with venom with every step he took.

"You know..." he continued, "Fae are generally protected in a way their powers cannot be taken unless we really try. But I swear, I'm really curious about you. The fact that you're a changeling, how you were initially a mortal and now have purple streaks in your hair. Now I just feel like hurting you for the feel of it, simply because I want to..."

"Haha, try me, sweetheart."

"And I know what your next few lines are gonna be, 'how do you know about me?'" He imitated my voice in an immature sound.

"And the answer to that is, I have my sources."

# CHAPTER 8

# Fire! Flames! Fame!

A week of pure torture goes by, but there's something good I have to tell you. I didn't cry. I didn't scream. I bit my tongue, clenched my teeth together, and held in my whimpers. My stomach hurt, and I had limited to no water and food. I was very fatigued. 'Revenge is a dish best served cold' I repeated to myself as an affirmation, along with "Karma exists."

But trust me, it gets better; keep listening.

I eventually got depressed and sick of the pain and torture, and listen closely when I tell you some details are best left unheard by you. It got worse and worse and worse, until one fine day...

"How's our little weakness doing?" Corvidus asked me in front of the secret circle members.

"I haven't cried or screeched or screamed. What makes you think you can break me now or anytime soon?"

"Faith, love. Faith."

"I'll say what I said a week back. **Try me.**"

"You've gotten used to my sarcasm and sadism, haven't you?" Corvidus grinned.

"I have. A skill very much necessary to survive."

He grinned harder.

Corvidus turned around and took some Scelena in his hands from the torturing table, turned back to face me, and said, "Get me a glass of water," He said to one of the members of the secret circle.

"Now!"

She returned with the water and a spoon.

He took the glass and mixed the Scelena with the water and brought the glass to me, making me sip on the water and pushing the rim of the glass to my mouth. He then forced me to chug the water down, and I did so, feeling an insane burning and stinging sensation in my throat and stomach, sort of like after when you throw up and your throat stings and burns. I was trying so hard to keep the Scelena-water mixture down, but it just wouldn't stay in my body, and as soon as he removed the glass from my mouth, I vomited all over the floor. A lot.

My throat burned even more. I didn't even think that was possible.

My eyes suddenly burned and stung, and all I knew next was that I was transforming into something else. My insides wanted to break free from the rest of my body. I felt like I was turning inside-out. That was when I burst free into a magical creature. I looked at my hands, my legs, I had scales, they were iridescent, they were purple. I had a long tongue. I had spikes covering my body. I was a dragon!

Corvidus was prepared for this very moment. I finally realized what he was trying to do. He was trying to abuse me so he could break me into my magical form and figure out what I was. He succeeded. After everything I tried and did, he still won.

I burst free and used this shapeshifting to my advantage to escape. But before I did so, I tried to breathe fire onto him. I didn't know how to; I just imagined breathing out through my mouth. The first try, it didn't work. The second try, it didn't work. The third try was the charm. I breathed fire right at his face. But just before my fire could reach him, he smiled evilly and swirled into a cyclone of ravens, guess that's where his name comes from. Corvidus - as in 'Corvids' or 'Corvidae,' a family of crows and ravens.

Shit! I missed my chance to hurt him. But I'll get it back, my chance. Instead, I used my newly formed body to escape. I grew so big within seconds that everyone looked microscopic to me. I tried flying, and surprisingly, it worked. It felt like flapping my arms back and forth and spreading them out. It was easy, but BALANCE - that was hard. I flew up, up, up, trying to enjoy this moment, not knowing if it will ever come back. I flew left, right, through clouds and mist in the air. Breathing fire once more out of excitement. It felt amazing, as though I was on top of the world, which I literally was. I felt spectacular, and felt at home in this body. I looked at myself and saw purple and black all over me. A little bit of green as well. *I knew I was a dragon; I didn't need a mirror to see it, I just knew.*

Since I was so high up in the air, I was able to see where I was going. Viridesca's castle was easy to spot further in the distance.

But I couldn't fly anymore. I was tired, hungry, and my stomach ached like hell. So I stopped at a forest near the castle (not the one I stayed in with my cabin, this forest was on the other end of the kingdom) and steep down. I didn't realize it then, and I sure as hell didn't know what was wrong with me, but I craved a deer to eat. And that was exactly what I saw from a point in the forest a few minutes after I settled in a comfy spot near the large Gulmohar trees. I was unable to turn back into a human. I tried, but I didn't know what exactly to try, so I failed. I didn't know how I turned into a dragon in the first place; I think the anger toward Corvidus got to me and was the trigger. But right then all I could feel was hunger. Insane starvation led to this.

I stalked the deer. I slowly treaded up to it with the pitter-patter of my legs, and my insane dragon instincts took over in less than a second. My mouth just clasped the deer in its grip, and I bit into the deer. The blood of the deer trickled down my throat, and my temptation and hunger grew. I chewed the deer and practically ate it. I was stunned with myself. *WHAT HAVE I DONE?* Is all I thought over and over again. But the deed was done, and I could honestly say that that was the best snack (not a meal) I'd had in decades.

The rain started pouring soon after I devoured the deer. It started off as a drizzle and eventually led to a thunderstorm.

The purple lightning was a beautiful sight in the sky. I felt like I was heard by nature. I felt wonderful, but guilty. Poor, sad, little snack of a deer. I hope it rests in peace. I laughed in my head, I tried laughing in person, but my mind would only whisper the laugh, and fire would spit out of my mouth. It made no sense. I didn't understand any of it. Was I a dragon now? Not fae? This may explain the purple streaks in my hair. But as much as I enjoyed being who I was, I had no idea how to turn back into a human, and that was a problem. BIG TIME.

I rested for a while and ate two more deer while I was at it. I'm quite good at stalking animals, if I do say so myself.

I eventually decided to go to Christopher in Viridesca's castle and seek his help. *He'll know what to do, he'll have the right people to reverse the change.* I thought to myself.

But as I came down to land in front of the castle, people (guards) and other Fae screamed and ran from me. I mean, I know the sight is not the best, but geez, at least show **some** form of respect.

They all ran inside the castle, but it was useless. I mean, if I wanted to, I could breathe fire and kill them all in a second. But I couldn't, moreover, I wouldn't!

The guards entered the castle and came back out with guns and swords and chains. "What type of monstrosity is this?!" I could hear a guard whisper. It was probably a shout, but given how high up in the air my head was, it was a whisper to me. "A mythical creature! A Wyvern!" Hardly NOT! I thought to myself. A wyvern has two legs and is much smaller than a dragon (and weaker in my opinion). How did I even know this? Damn, me and my high IQ.

"What is this? Or perhaps who is it? A Fae turned into a wyvern?" Another guard said. *Why do people keep calling me a Wyvern?!*

I tried turning back into my human form again, like I had practiced in the forest, but to no avail.

They started pointing the guns at me, and as I backed up, Bam! Bullets straight at my stomach. Um. Ow?!

More guns pointed toward my stomach, they probably thought my dragon form was pregnant because my stomach was severely bloated from all the acidity due to lack of food.

The bullets actually started hurting after a bit, and they were all embedded into the thick skin of my flesh. Alright, time to stop. I breathed fire at the guards in self-defense, which only seemed to worsen the problem.

CHAPTER 9

# Safe

More bullets tore through my skin, some of them silver, some of them wooden. I assumed nobody (including myself) actually knew how to hurt me. Nothing they tried worked, until I started feeling a heavy weight on my wings. Chains. Thick, hard, metallic chains. But if that were the only case, why did they sting and burn? **Scelena.** They were coated with Scelena.

I was caught and tied together with almost a group of what looked like fifty to a hundred guards. It took the entire lot to at least get me controlled and calmed down. The chains started piercing through my flesh and thick scaly skin. I was bound by the Scelena-coated chains. I passed out from the pain.

The next thing I knew, I was waking up in a cage. A cage outside, right in front of the castle, for everyone to look at. Everyone was staring at me – all types of Fae. Men, women, children. They were all taken aback by my dragon form. Finally settling on the fact that I'm not a wyvern and am, in fact, a dragon.

Then what I saw was remarkable. Not in the best way, in the worst way. People were paying money to see me on display. I was shocked to my core. What type of immature and torturous behavior was Christopher allowing to happen?! After all, he is the ruler of this kingdom!

I then saw Christopher coming outside and yelling at the guards, people, and army. But I couldn't make out what he was saying. I'm too tall and high up in the air to make out the soft voices. He then stared into my eyes with an angry look that slowly dissipated into warmth as tears streamed down my dragon face. People started collecting the large drops in a giant metallic tub.

I then realized that in ancient Viridescan mythology, dragon tears are said to contain ingredients that, when mixed with certain magical herbs, possess healing properties. They were all taking advantage of me! That was when I suddenly melted with Chris's look and turned back into a human. My hair was disheveled, my eyes watery and purple, my clothes half torn to pieces. Everyone looked at me with a hint of amusement as well as surprise in their eyes. They knew now. They all knew now.

Christopher quickly unlocked the cage and pulled me out before hugging me tight. He was crying as he said, "I'm sorry. You didn't deserve what my men did to you; I had no idea of this! I had no part in this. I hope you believe me." I cried onto his shoulders as I said, "I know, I know." He then took me inside the castle and took me to my guest room. He allowed me to rest, gave me a blanket, a change of clothes, and told me to rest up. He told me, "I know that you're tired, but we have to talk."

"Later…" I groaned sleepily.

He looked at me with tension in his eyes and then closed the door and left. After an hour of sleeping, I took a quick shower, and it was dinner time. I strode down to the dining room and saw Chris sitting at the edge of the table. I said, "Hi." I had no idea what else to say, all things considered. He realized this by taking one look at my face and said, "Hi." back. I settled into the table and started eating the cheese sandwiches that were placed on the table.

"How are you?" He asked.

"Better," I replied.

"Ready to talk?"

"Ready," I confidently said after sighing.

He then proceeded to talk to me about what happened and asked me how I transformed into a dragon.

"Corvidus caught me. He threatened my parents."

"I thought you didn't like your parents..."

"I don't. I didn't. But They're still people, they've never committed a sin or a crime, besides well, you know, treating me the way they did. Regardless, they are still people, they had to be saved."

"I understand..." He took in a deep breath before saying, "what happened next?"

"Scelena right?"

"Yes? What do you mean?"

"It's called Scelena, right?"

"He used that against me, he threw it in my face."

**"He did not!"**

"He did..."

The conversation continued, and I stopped talking when he was all caught up. Eventually, he started talking again. I think the shock got to him.

"People will start seeing you as a threat."

"So?"

"What do you mean 'so'?"

"So what? It's not like we can do anything about it..."

I sipped my rose lemonade and slurped up the last few drops of it through my straw.

"We can. There's an option."

"What?" I asked.

"There's an elite academy called Alexandrite Academy, where they teach people like you that aren't exactly Fae, but that are other magical creatures, how to control their powers and how to use it to their advantage. People will be after your rare, magical tears and magic as a dragon and will do anything, ANYTHING, to claim it. Even though I am royalty, they won't listen to me. You saw how they treated you without even taking my consent. There's no other choice," he said sternly.

"Go on..."

"In this academy, you will be treated as an equal. You will be helped, especially if I put in a word..."

I sighed. I started to protest, but then I quickly came to my senses and realized I couldn't do anything about this. The best thing to do was to protect myself, and the more I stayed at Viridesca, the more pressure I put on Chris to take care of me.

# Chapter 10
# Alexandrite Academy

So I joined this so-called elite academy, 'Alexandrite Academy,' which wasn't too far from Viridesca but far enough and secluded enough that nobody would be able to find me or the other students. It was protected by some sort of magical barrier, so only known and allowed people/Fae could enter. We had to travel to Alexandrite Academy by boat; it was situated on an island. We got ready and started rowing, and that was when…

"Umm, Chris?" My body was slowly starting to shake, and I got goosebumps.

"Yeah? Whoa, why are you shaking?"

"Behind you." I looked ahead of him with my eyes wide open and gestured to the monster lurking beneath the ocean with my eyes.

"What the—"

Bam! A hit to the boat from underneath.

"Chris, what do we do? What is that thing?"

It looked a lot like the Loch Ness monster, like a water-dragon. Chris quickly explained to me and said that it's called a Hydra-Serpent.

He told me that it has a cave where it generally resides and only comes out when sensing competition or threats. "I guess he must have sensed that you're a dragon?"

"Is that even possible?"

"Yeah. Each creature has a unique scent. You must have a unique dragon scent on you."

Bam! Another hit.

"Christopher, we need to act fast."

"Can you reach Alexandrite Academy on your own by transforming into a dragon and flying there? I can then come safely as the threat will be gone for the Hydra-serpent."

I sighed. "I can try."

I closed my eyes and focused all my energy on turning into a dragon. With a lot of mental maneuvering, it finally worked.

I grew and grew and grew and breathed fire. I flew away from the boat and reached the academy within seconds, at that height.

I landed in the forest behind the academy and changed my form into a human somehow by focusing my thoughts, and then fell to the ground and fainted.

After a while, Christopher found me and resuscitated me by giving me some water and working with his Fae magic. As soon as Chris and I reached Alexandrite Academy, he left me to fend for myself. A guy, around my age, named Landon, was the one who was assigned to me by Chris, and Christopher told him to show me around and introduce me to the situation at the academy.

He basically helped me get accustomed to the school campus. I got to my dorm eventually, on the east side of the academy, and found my roommates to be quite nice. I was also measured for my uniform and was told that I would be receiving my uniform the next day.

I took this opportunity to my advantage and decided to start getting to know my fellow roommates and to start socializing if I truly wanted to fit in here.

That being said, it wasn't all that easy to get to know people. Beside my roommates, of course. Three people living with me in that one tiny accommodation. Dara, a short girl with hazelnut hair and a pixie cut, a smile that piqued my curiosity, and a muscular build. Michelle, too girly for me, blonde and blue-eyed. And finally, Taylor, my favorite. Sparkly eyes would not begin to describe the best of her. She had long brown hair, and her style was somewhere in between that of Dara's and Michelle's.

We finally started to get to know each other and eventually got to my very first class. But before that, orientation. During orientation, a teacher started stating that there were two types of classes. One was all about verbal magic and spells, the other was all about physical training. It was annoying to hear about, especially after she went on about these two for a very long time. You may say, "What do you mean by 'a very long time'?" Well, I mean two damn hours. Two DAMN HOURS! She also specified that the school was made for special creatures like us to awaken and help fight off Fleskies if they target us, which they will apparently, so, no pressure.

Anyways, the rest of my first day went by quite quickly after that orientation session. Landon asked me if I needed help with anything else, and I proudly and confidently said, "No thanks." I really did spend my time wisely on my first day. I looked around the school and spent my time getting to know the faculty and other students in my grade, although I didn't get along with them as well as I had hoped to.

I slept soundly that night, knowing that I was in safe hands, and so was Christopher. He was safe in his own kingdom. My first day of "classes" began the next day. Of course, classes had started way before as well; after all, I was late in joining the academy, and so were a couple of other students for whom the orientation session was held the day before. I just spent my first day there not putting too much pressure on myself and by using time to settle into the area. After a while, I finally gave myself permission to start the classes.

In my first class, four important aspects of magic were taught: shapeshifting, element control, super hearing, and super speed. It started off simple, with element control. It was supposed to be easier than the other classes. We were told to quickly settle down at our desks and then were brought some soil, water, and a matchstick and matchbox each. We were supposed to try to change each element into the opposite element and let the teacher know when we succeeded.

It was going to get more difficult, or so we were told. Lessons on changing each element into all three other elements besides just the opposite element were our proceeding class next week. Then, we also had to learn to conjure up each element on our own and finally learn how to use those elements to either help and save others (for healing) or for battle and protection against our enemies. I tried my best, you must believe me because I really did, but nothing, and I mean absolutely **nothing**, worked.

I couldn't change each element into the opposite one. In fact, when the other students could begin their work, I had no idea where to even start. Did I need to use my hands, my palms? Or my mind and eyes? Did I have to touch the elements or just play around? I had no idea where to begin. And there went the bell, the alarm for my next class. I packed up whatever scraps of materials I had squished in my bag and left.

Here's what really annoyed me though… Apparently, I was a bit more, well, let's use the term "special" than the others. There were either different types of Fae or maybe Centaurs, Griffins, Vampires, and Mermaids, while I, *sigh*, was a dragon.

So, it was a little harder to fit in than you would expect. What makes me say that? Well, I could **hear** whispers and see side eyes (yes, I could literally hear side eyes) in the halls of the school and around the campus.

The next class on my timetable was sparring. SPARRING?! I am not a physical exercise kind of person; I'm not even a physical kind of person. To me, I just live in my head.

*Great, here goes nothing!*

As soon as I got to the Sparring class, we were told to change out of our uniforms into a more comfortable suit meant for sparring. I took pride in being the first person popping out of the change room, ready to start the class before the others. But I could sense danger, a problem coming. It wasn't a type of danger that I was so used to back at my house; this was more of a danger I was ready to **not** run from. The feeling just made me want to bite back at the danger I saw coming. I couldn't identify my danger. Nothing of the obvious made me identify why I was ready to pounce. But then it struck me! A boy, no older than 19, saw me and gave me a death stare. I only noticed it then, but it seemed like he had been staring at me for decades, and I just didn't pay attention.

The teacher told us first-years to stand in a single line and fight with whatever knowledge we had of sparring with the person standing opposite us, who was apparently from the second year in this school. At one point, it was my turn, and guess who I had to spar with?

That's right! Death stare boy.

"Ready? Set? SPAR!" The teacher yelled. There he was, staring at me in the most uncomfortable manner. He gave me the stink eye. Exhausting. Just fess up already! 'Okay fine, you're my sparring partner, I'm your sparring partner, let's just get this over with.'

The instructor spoke up at that moment: "READY? SET. SPAR!"

He took that initial moment of space and me spacing out as an excuse to hit me. And he did. Whoosh! The air made a sound.

I was hit right in the face. "Okay, **what** is wrong with you?"

"Just doing what we're here for, little one."

"Oh, so we have nicknames now?" I looked at the instructor and gave an eye movement that clearly said, "Do you see what I see?".

SLAP! Another hit. "Well, I have a nickname for you if that's what you were asking..." BAM! Another hit. This time in my stomach. "What are you doing! This is against the rules. This isn't sparring!"

"Okay enough," the instructor stated. "This is not right, Aretos. You can't go against the rules." "Alright," he said, quietly, morbidly. I took this moment where he paused to my advantage and kicked him in the shin.

He didn't flinch, let alone whimper or cry. He just stood there and grinned back, evilly.

"I'm going to go out on a limb here and say you don't have any experience with self-defense." "You're right, I don't," I replied back, hastily. "But I have seen many movies and read many books on how to spar without going against the rules."

"Man, you sure know how to bore a person with long sentences."

"Enough talking, we need more action going on, especially if you're to prepare for the worst..." The instructor hastened.

"Please, ladies first," Axel Aretos stated.

"Wow? Did I just hear a 'please' come from that mouth of yours?"

"It isn't that surprising. Is it?"

"Think fast!" I swiped at his head with a quick movement.

He dodged at me, coming for my head instead, aiming and swiping again.

But here's the thing, I wasn't expecting that. I got too caught up in the antics of it all, that I didn't anticipate what was going to come. And there went my entire body, twisting and falling to the ground.

My neck twisted so much with the amount of pressure he put into that hit that I couldn't turn it. Crap. Every movement I made, ached with pain and torture. I tried to stand up, but I just couldn't. "Um, a little help please?" I almost certainly begged the instructor. He wasn't even paying attention, though, minding his own business, talking to someone else. But you know who was paying attention? That's right, Aretos. He showed me his hand and was supposedly trying to help me get up? I don't even know to this day if that was his true intention, but dumbfoundedly, I took it. He pulled me up hastily.

I squealed in pain and whimpered. Tears started pooling in my eyes. God, no. This wasn't supposed to be happening. "You good?" he asked.

"Um, no. I don't think so?"

"Sir? She needs to see a doctor or at least a nurse." The instructor's eyes were immediately on Aretos. *Wow, how partial could he even be? He didn't give a hoot when I was on the ground, but now that Aretos is speaking, all eyes are on him?*

Psycho. Literal Psycho.

But I mean, he did help me when Aretos was hitting me and making movements against the rules...

What—okay, we gotta get a move on with this story; there's still a lot to say...

"What's wrong, Aretos?"

"She's injured. Or sprained. I don't know, either way, she needs to see somebody who can help."

All this while he was still holding me in his arms. And all this while I had no idea who he even was. What's happening? Was all that went into my head.

"You'll need to take her; none of us instructors are available, and everyone else needs to spar."

Aretos sighed. "Fine."

He let go of my back, and I fell again. He cursed. He said, "Don't overthink what I'm about to do; it's just faster and I have things to do." And without warning, he lifted me up by the back of my legs and swooped me in his arms. I squealed. He practically strolled and reached the nurse's office within minutes, nevertheless.

He laid me on the bed harshly, and a whisper of "thanks" escaped my mouth. "Whatever," he said grinning, and he left just after saying, "Oh, and we need to talk, dorm room 137. Whenever you're ready." Great. What am I to do with all this idle curiosity laying around?

The nurse helped with my back and gave me a soothing balm along with some medicines. But since I was in an exceptionally bad state, she said she had to use magic to get me walking again. "What does tha- *hisses in pain*"

"Fair warning: this might sting."

It took me an hour, but eventually, I could stand, and eventually walk. And what better time than now to meet Aretos about what he wanted to "talk" about. I headed to his dorm room after circling the place almost three times and getting lost. I knocked and put my ears to the door. "Aretos? You wanted to talk?"

"Give me a minute, Freya."

*Whoa. He's never called me that before. How does he even know my name? Something must be seriously wrong...*

He said this with an exceptionally stern voice. I waited patiently. Unlike myself. He eventually opened the door, and a woman came out. The head of the school. "Miss, I'm sorry, I was unaware of your presence." I was loud, clear, and confident. But I was wondering how informal this meeting could have been if it was held in Aretos' room, with the door shut? Aretos looked concerned when she left.

"What's happeni-" he pulled me in and locked the door before casting a magic spell to create a secret, invisible orb where we couldn't be heard.

## Chapter 11

# Amulet

"Umm, what's happening?"

"I needed to talk to you, remember? Isn't that why you came here in the first place?"

"Yeah, but do we really need this bubble? What is so secretive that people might attempt to hear even behind closed doors?"

"So, here's the thing, I'm assigned to be your trainer, your teacher, and to help you awaken."

"Awaken? Did you really just say 'awaken'?"

"Yeah, I did. I'm not playing around, Freya."

"How do you know my name?" Shit was getting suspicious.

"I know everything about you. Dragon shifter."

"**Okay**. Bye."

I turned around to leave, but as I was about to walk out the door, Aretos grabbed my arm and whirled me back to face him.

"So here's what's going to happen. Apparently, you're one of the special ones, which I'm finding really difficult to understand, but... you are. So I'm supposed to help you become your truest self and help you shift into a dragon as easily as breathing."

"But why you? Really? I mean, they couldn't find someone else a little nicer, maybe even interesting?"

"Gee, thanks. But I feel the exact same way about you too, you know?"

I sighed and said, "So what's the procedure?"

"This ain't rocket science; I can take care of a little girl."

"Excuse me! I'm as old as you are, well, almost. And I don't need 'taking care' of."

"Sure, you don't," Aretos smiled.

He paused, then smirked. *Ugh. This guy can really be a douche sometimes.*

Anyways, a week went by in peace. It's true. I wasn't disturbed, not even by Aretos, and I found my way around the boundless school. Fortunately, I made one or two friends. Unfortunately though, I made more than one or two enemies too. And since this was a school all about magic... I wondered whether they would use that to their advantage to strike.

And then they did. The next day that I woke up, well, I screamed. I was looking for my clothes to get dressed, and I realized that they weren't where I left them. Okay, fine, no big deal, I'll just reach into my cupboard and get out some new clothes and find these ones later. But as soon as I looked into my cupboard, I found cockroaches in place of my clothes and quite literally freaked the fuck out.

*Oh my god. They're dead meat!*

Was all I could repeat to myself in hopes of calming myself down. I had my PJs on, but now I had to leave the room with my pajamas to look for, or at least get new clothes. But the school was huge, so I couldn't possibly go around the entire hallway searching for my clothes.

I had to settle for an option a little less traumatizing than this. Asking **him** for help. He's the only one not in practice right now and the only one, quite frankly, on the entire floor level of my dorm. So I quietly moved toward his room and knocked on the door once, hard. He opened the door and broke into a cacophony of laughter. Jeez.

"Shhhhh. So you know my current state? Willing to help out a girl a little?"

"What the hell happened?" he continued laughing.

"They stole my clothes."

"Who?"

"I don't know! Okay, I don't know their names, but my enemies, they stole my clothes, okay?"

"I thought I was your enemy..."

"If you don't end up helping me out, you'll end up being more than just my enemy." I gave Aretos a withering stare.

"At least tell me what they look like?" He asked gently. Before I could get a chance to respond, we could hear mysterious giggling coming from the end of the hallway. Uh-oh.

"It's them," I whispered.

"Hold tight," he said, and proceeded to glide over toward them smoothly after which he started smacking them left and right, kicking them, and throwing punches.

"What's your name?" My enemy started whimpering... "Silas."

"Where are her clothes? I'm giving you a minute to answer. If I don't get a response from you by then, or let's say I do get a response but it's false, then I'm just going to have to find new and improved ways to torture you. Finger-breaking, perhaps?"

Wow. He actually. Wow. They then told him where they hid my clothes; they were whispering and whimpering so much I could barely hear them, and I went into my room to just sit in silence until Aretos finished… whatever was happening out there. Damn.

Aretos returned after a few minutes with my clothes on his bloodied hands and said, "Sorry you had to see that."

"There are other ways to deal with people than violence, you know?"

"I know," was all he said before he left. The next few hours were quite painful. Literally. I had trouble focusing in class, so I missed the next few classes of the day, including Sparring practice.

I was prepared for the 'abandonment' lecture I was gonna get from Aretos. I headed back to my room and spent the rest of the time in my bed, curled up inside my blanket like a tortilla. I was in tears, my stomach was cramping like never before, and weirdly, I felt like throwing up. I hadn't felt this much pain in my upper stomach for a while. And it didn't feel gastric. It felt like something I'd never felt before.

Unusual. During the last school hour of the day, Aretos barged into my room and pinned me to the wall against my neck and screamed into my face. "I'm supposed to be taking care of you! Protecting you, in case you turn into a dragon! What if it happened here? Today? I would be treated as dead to the faculty. Where have you been, Freya?"

"In pain," I replied, trembling and with labored breathing following my next few whispers. "Violence isn't the answer to everything. If you know, then why are you like this?"

"Pain? What do you mean?" I fell to the floor in tears. "I don't know what's wrong with me. I've never felt this way before! What the hell is happening to me?"

"Freya, talk to me. Tell me what's going on!"

"My stomach, my chest, my heart, it all hurts!"

"Is it?"

"NO!" I stopped him before he could say much else or finish his sentence. "No, it's not," I replied, my voice husky.

"Oh my god," Aretos was in shock. "What?"

"You're transforming! It'll take some time from here, but as far as I know, this might be the initial stages of pain felt from your transformation process beginning."

"But I was able to transform before without pain."

"How many times have you transformed?"

"Twice," I whispered.

"Yeah, that doesn't count. This pain is happening because of the final stage in the process of beginning your transformation."

"Wait, what. You're just confusing me!"

"It doesn't matter. Just follow my lead."

He pushed a stray hair behind my ear and told me to get some rest because tomorrow was apparently gonna be a 'long day.' His words, not mine. The next day, during the middle of my second class, I felt immense pain again. Same place, different time. Heart, chest, upper stomach. I couldn't breathe. I felt like my windpipe was being crushed.

I quickly excused myself from class and dialed Aretos' number on my phone. The pain this time was unbearable. It was really, really gut-wrenchingly excruciating!

He picked up. "Talk," he said.

"It's happening."

"Where are you?"

"Outside Ms. Madison's class."

"I'll be there in 2 minutes. Hang tight."

He reached within a minute and grabbed my hand and sprinted outside. I gagged and ran over to a bush to throw up. My puke was purple and glittery. "WHOA," I was starstruck.

The next minute, everything went blurry, and my pupils dilated. A lot of brightness was entering my eyes. "I'm right here. If you need me." Aretos held me again and then let go of my hand.

Suddenly, I feel every muscle and bone in my body tearing and breaking, and I scream in agonizing pain. I curl up and almost fall when I suddenly shift my form into a large dragon.

The wings are webbed and large,

The skin scaly and shining in iridescent purple.

I grow, I keep growing until I'm larger than the entire length of the school.

All this while, while I was transforming, Aretos smiled and looked like he was feeling proud? Weird.

Really weird.

I suddenly then transform into a human again with torn and ripped clothes and then transform into a dragon again, all in a single minute.

This keeps happening, and Aretos stands by and watches, and LAUGHS. That asshole. He doesn't even try to help me, but then at one point while I'm human, I try to talk and yell at him to help me, which only gets conveyed blatantly.

He eventually reaches out and gives me a necklace, later known to me as a magical shifting-control amulet. I put it on quickly when I'm human, and I maintain my posture as a human. I don't shift into a dragon again. I'm human this time, and I remain human.

He explains to me that I'll remain human as long as I wear the amulet, at least for the beginning stages of my new life as a dragon, up until I learn to control the shifting process on my own.

"Freya, Axel, meet me at my office. Now," our principal called out to us on the field.

"We'll be there," I replied, tired and sore from the pain that I just went through.

We then proceeded to walk into the office, looking confused, concerned, and alert.

"Ah. You're here. Please, have a seat, the both of you," our principal's voice was low and quite ominous.

Me and Axel, we both looked at each other and then sat down silently.

"So, you've shifted." Well, that was straightforward.

"Yes, I guess?... I'm sorry, what exactly is this meeting about?" I asked.

"We need to know about your parents. It's imperative, for, you know, the school."

"I'm sorry, how is this related to the school?"

"Just tell me, and don't shy away from what I'm about to tell you."

"By all means, go ahead."

"Do you, by any chance, have an idea of who your real parents are? We have to know if there are more dragons, as you have been the first one, there could just as well be others too. What do you think?"

"I... I don't know what to think." I was starting to feel faint from the physical exertion on my body. It was noticeable.

Aretos started speaking. "Maybe we should give her some time, to, you know, adjust to the new changes."

"Right, of course, just a couple more things.

1. Mr. Aretos, you need to guard her now at all times, and this has to become your first priority. This is very important as we have heard from our students that they all feel threatened by her.
2. Everyone is afraid of you, Freya. Dragons have been a myth for a long time, and I don't think many of our faculty members and students are ready to accept you as being our first-ever sighted dragon. You need to lie low for some time. Your enemies will be after you, and no matter how many school rules we place, they will break it because they are all equally frightened by you." A pause. "No one really expected you to turn into a dragon; I guess most of us were in denial."

Our principal paused and took a deep breath before continuing. "And finally, 3- Axel, you need to start her special training so that she learns how to fly and control other aspects of her dragon form."

"So, we can leave now?" I asked in a begrudging tone.

"Yes, you're dismissed."

CHAPTER 12

# Prom? Prom.

A couple of months went by with special training given to me by Aretos. He dropped some of his classes so he could spend more time taking care of my dragon form and preparing me for battle. Battle against our enemies. Yes, my enemies have now become our enemies.

Anyway, I woke up and went to class where prom was starting to be discussed. I really didn't support the idea of prom. I started to feel like it was kind of childish and didn't really want to partake in these events. But my friends felt like they really wanted to participate and wanted me involved. So, after finally agreeing, they decided to take me shopping at the end of the day.

The day came to an end quite quickly. We got special permission to head out of the academy to go shopping for prom. We headed to a boutique in Sugar Hill, New

Hampshire and decided to browse through all the dresses.

"Hey, Freya! This looks quite nice," Taylor pointed at a red dress that was very simple but elegant.

"Yeah, red's not really my color," I replied.

"What about this one? I think green's your color," Dara and Michelle pointed at a green, embroidered, sparkly, glittery dress.

"Too much?" Dara asked.

"Nope, just right for me? After all, aren't I too much?"

We all laughed and continued shopping for the others.

As we headed to a coffee shop to stop for some snacks, we saw Axel and some of his friends having suits in their hands and smiling and talking.

It's a small town, I was bound to run into him at some point. I was wondering who was going to be my date for the prom. I didn't want to go in the first place, I sure as hell wasn't going to end up there alone.

I thought I should ask him, but I'm sure it's a given because he's been spending time with me all throughout these past few months.

Alright, let's just leave it be was all that went through my mind while another part of me was saying confirm it. Ask him. It'll be more embarrassing for you to assume he'll be your date and then imagine him ending up going with someone else.

I decided to listen to the first part of my mind.

We ended up paying for the coffee and seeing Axel and his guy friends leaving.

So, the prom eventually arrives, and the night before, I fell asleep early and missed dinner because I was feeling tired, and besides, I wasn't really hungry. I woke up again at what felt like midnight but kept my eyes closed, trying to get some sleep. I saw someone enter my room and could see a shadow of a guy. I sat up straight in bed after opening my eyes.

"Hi," I say.

"Hey," Axel says back.

"So?"

"The prom?"

"I know this is going to be awkward, so let me make it easier for you. I'll be accompanying you as your date, so I'd better not see another guy bringing you so much as a corsage."

"Hey! You may have the responsibility of taking care of me and training me, but you don't get to decide who I go with or spend my time with."

"I do. I follow rules. You're just another rule to me."

"Oh, is that all I am?"

"I didn't mea-"

"Get out."

"I'm sorry." Aretos left and shut the door behind him.

Later, a little early in the morning, I could hear Axel talking to his friends while his friends were mansplaining stuff to my friends outside, and I eavesdropped - "Her life is rare. Don't touch her or even dare to go near her, she must be protected. She's a rare species."

"Don't worry, we'll leave your little princess Freya alone."

CHAPTER 13

# The Beginning

It was time for the prom.

There was a large staircase leading to the main foyer.

I took a deep breath and started walking down the stairs in my green dress with my hair in an updo consisting of jewels.

I could see eyes wide open and hear gasps of surprise and awe.

I saw Axel Aretos standing at the bottom of the stairs, waiting for me with a corsage and an arm out and folded. What is it with him and corsages? I laughed in my head.

I held his hand and looked around while my dress flowed freely on the dance floor.

Everyone moved away from me in what I assumed was fear, but I decided to start embracing that side of me. So, I walked with confidence instead of sadness and embarrassment.

"You look lovely."

"Why thank you, you do too."

"A man looks lovely to you?"

"Stop being sexist, Axel."

He lifted his hands up in an "okay then" motion.

We danced to various songs on the dance floor; I actually ended up having fun!

"Didn't know you were NOT such a snooze fest."

"I could say the same about you, Freya."

"Then say it."

We danced until our legs felt numb.

I went over to the bar and drank a couple of margaritas and some ginger shots.

Everything I remember from there is a blur, but based on what Aretos told me, it seemed as though I danced on a couple of tables and had a lot of fun.

That was up until I drank some water and sobered up.

The next thing I knew, I could hear a sharp scratching or cutting noise, what sounded like blades on the ceiling up above, and could see diamonds falling off the chandeliers.

Within the blink of an eye, I saw Corvidus. *Wait what-Corvidus?!*

YES. CORVIDUS. He jumped from a large metallic scorpion with blades for legs and landed on the dance floor. The entire party fell to complete pin-drop silence.

"Hello, Freya."

I had tears in my eyes.

The scorpion started killing people all around me.

ALL I could hear were screams, and I could only see blood splattered everywhere.

Axel told me to get to safety and hide somewhere, while he would target and kill the spider, "Be safe," I told him, to which he replied with "Don't come out until I find you!" and ran, after grabbing a sword from the weapons section which is there in every room, toward the spider.

I sprinted while holding up my dress, and my hair started falling out of the updo and came half undone.

I went into the bathroom and hid there, standing above the toilet and whimpering and trembling in fear.

I pinched myself in the hopes of waking up from what could possibly be a nightmare.

Nothing happened.

*This shit was real.*

A few minutes went by in absolute horror. I could hear nothing but screams and blood-curdling sounds. I could hear scratching and scraping noises again and again and again. The sounds were getting closer and closer to me. I started sobbing in fear. What the hell was I supposed to do?

The bathroom door opened with a creaking noise.

"Freya, come out, come out wherever you are..." I heard Corvidus' voice and held in my pleas for help so he could somehow not find me. Now that I look back on this, I, quite frankly, don't know what I was thinking.

I could hear the doors of each bathroom stall being opened and broken and thrashed onto the floor.

I got so scared my breathing started to become heavy, and that gave away my voice. I was having a panic attack.

## Chapter 14

# Back to Sugar Hill

The next thing I know, Corvidus burst into the door of the bathroom stall I'm in and says, "Finally! Cheeky little one, aren't you? You do know how to get away when the time calls for it. But that won't last."

He grabbed my arm, and we suddenly disappeared into thin air. I had no idea where we were headed, but I thought it best not to provoke him by asking him questions he won't give me answers to.

I couldn't help myself. We reappeared in the middle of a forest in God-knows-where, and I immediately asked him, "Why the hell did you take me here? Let me go!"

"Shut up."

I tried pulling my hand free from his, but his grip was iron-tight.

I started screaming for help.

"No one is here for miles. No one is going to help you. You can shut up and listen or we will have to do this the hard way."

"Fine. What do you want?"

"I'm going to give you an ultimatum. Help me kill my father, and then as a thank you, I'll allow you to rule Zantedeschia for as long as you live. As a dragon, of course."

"As a dragon? Do you even know how long dragons are supposed to live?"

"Yeah, like a million years or something."

"Make that a billion."

"Fine. I may give you some time to be human in between - but that's my final offer."

"Offer disrespectfully declined!"

"Think about this. You can rule by my side and be happy with all the riches in the kingdom of Zantedeschia."

"Not everything is about money."

"Wow. You're one of those."

"What?"

"Nothing, do you accept or not?"

"I told you, I DON'T. Now let me go, you prick."

I tried to change into the form of my dragon but to no avail. I couldn't take the amulet off for some godforsaken reason.

I had to remain human for as long as possible. I had to survive like this. I wasn't complaining. I'm better off not undergoing pain to transform into a dragon. But, Christ, *what do I do about Corvidus?*

"Okay, listen, I'll give you some time to reconsider my offer."

We could hear the crunching of the leaves as he walked toward a large rock topped with moss and sat down.

I tried to scream for help again, and I had no idea which way to go because it was a large, dense evergreen forest. I couldn't see anything for miles, just like he said.

"Keep trying to scream; eventually, your throat will go dry, **and** no one will come to help you. It's a win-win for me, you know?"

I was walking mindlessly through the forest in my green dress trying to think about what Corvidus would do if I declined his offer again. As I started walking, Corvidus got up from the rock and started following me. *Ugh.*

I wasn't going to listen to him anyway. I had to stand my ground.

Corvidus stopped following me after 20 minutes of both of us walking in silence, and he stepped in front of me, turning to look at my face.

"So. What do you say?"

"NO!" I kicked him and yelled at his face. "Take me back. NOW!"

"No. I disrespectfully decline." Oh my god. Did he just use my own line against me? That-!

He then grabbed my arm, and we teleported through his cyclone of ravens all the way to the location of the door in the middle of the forest.

He started telling me, "Sorry honey, but it's my way, or the highway."

To which I responded with, "How cliché can you even b—"

I started screaming. He pushed me with all his force into the other side of the door. I had no idea how I'd get back here, and trust me when I say, leaving wasn't an option.

I ended up at a bar in Sugar Hill, New Hampshire.

Everyone was staring at me with intense gazes. I stopped dead in my tracks, smiled, and waited for the questions to be thrown at me.

"How did she appear out of nowhere?"

"Who is she?"

"Shh."

I heard whispers, questions, and remarks of all kinds.

I simply ignored the questions and threw around sassy comebacks to those remarks which were rude, mean, and simply disrespectful.

They shut up.

Good, let them know I have a sharp tongue.

Here's the problem though: my amulet disappeared. It was the first thing I looked for when I reached the bar and the last thing I had on me.

But what's weird is that I didn't transform into a dragon. I was supposed to, without the amulet and all, but I didn't.

I left the place in a huff and decided to look for a place to stay, since I had no idea how long I'd be here.

But first, money. I had none.

I had to resort to the fun version of me getting my hands on some money: stealing.

Why? Because there wasn't a chance in hell I'd go to my adoptive parents. They wouldn't want me back, and trust me, I didn't want them back either.

I decided to look for something of value I could steal and then use that to stay at an apartment for a while. I found people walking around with jewels around their wrists and necks and ears in the form of jewelry.

It sounded hard, the idea of stealing, but I was sure that doing the actual deed couldn't be too difficult. And it was not. I was right.

I swiftly snatched the bracelets, necklaces, and earrings left and right.

I got a total of ten pieces of jewelry. Good. That should last me a while. I spent the rest of the night in a cheap motel called Midnight Motel as I couldn't find an apartment that I could rent temporarily.

They accepted the jewelry as payment at the front desk. I just hoped the psycho from the movie "Psycho" wouldn't come alive and end up slaughtering me in my sleep.

I continued to stay in the motel for the next few days, and on the night of the third day, I saw a couple of ravens sitting on a branch of a tree outside my room windowsill. They reminded me of Corvidus.

I got so angry, and my eyes started burning with rage that I threw my pillow (I was lying on my bed) onto the windowsill in the direction of the ravens.

I then suddenly saw a shadow just in front of the closed door of my room.

Shit.

CHAPTER 15

# You Really Hate Me, Don't You?

Immediately, I screamed in fear, and Corvidus made his grand appearance as usual. Ugh.

"Dude! You scared me!" I yelled at his face.

"That's kind of the point?" He smirked.

"Ugh. What do you want now? And where's my amulet?"

"Reconsider my offer."

I sighed and rolled my eyes before saying, "Or what, tough guy?"

"Or, I'll threaten your parents again and kill them."

My face got small and serious.

"Yeah, that's what I thought. You won't be hurt or affected directly, but your loved ones will..." Corvidus' words were laced with venom.

I thought for a moment, closed my eyes, then agreed.

"Fine. I'll help you."

Little did he know that I had a plan brewing. I was going to kill Corvidus after helping him to kill his father. *It's a classic two birds with one stone scenario. It could work!*

The minute I said that, we both disappeared into an array of darkness.

We reappeared in an essence or a void, perhaps, of iridescence.

Basically, that's just a fancy way of saying that we reappeared in the mountains.

Mountains that have never been seen before, mountains that were towering over us, and mountains that were literally glittery.

"Welcome to Evermist," Corvidus proudly stated.

"What the—" I turned around wheeling in all directions. Where the hell was I?

And why was this place so beautiful? So mystical? So magical? In fact, it felt mythical.

After taking a few minutes to - adjust - I would say, to the new environments... Corvidus whistled, and immediately his little scorpion blade thingy appeared.

I jumped back in alarm.

"Whoa, whoa, easy boy," Corvidus said.

"If you let that thing even within a meter from me, I will legitimately kill you."

"You can sure try.

Don't worry, he won't hurt you until he is ordered to do so. So you'd better remain on my good side." Corvidus winked.

I rolled my eyes.

"Why is he even here?"

"To help us practice."

"Practice? What are you talking about?"

"Think fast!" Corvidus threw my amulet into the air in my direction, and I quickly bent down to catch it.

"You've had it this whole time? Prick!"

"Yeah, wanted to see the look on your face when you realized what you just realized..."

"I'm going to kill you." I started pacing toward him when he said, "Uh-uh." And smiled when I realized that he sent the scorpion after me.

Bitch.

I stopped moving, closed my eyes, and waited for the scorpion to leave. It eventually did.

"Let's start training, enough games," Corvidus stated abruptly.

"You really need me to train to kill your father? I'm a badass dragon; I could kill him in a heartbeat."

He smiled.

"That's what you think, but he's not so easily killable."

"Fine. Let's get this over with."

"Here." He held out a sword.

I grabbed it with a swift move. "What now?" I asked him.

He used his sword to clash with mine, but it really felt like he was aiming for my head instead.

"Now, we fight." We continued our training of sword-fighting for the next hour or so. It felt really weird. I was training with one of my greatest enemies; that's so not normal.

I could only hear my ragged breathing and the sounds of our swords clashing against each other.

After an hour went by, I was dripping sweat, and so was Corvidus.

We then took a break, drank some water from the water springs and fountains in the mountains and started fighting again. This time without swords, instead with our hands. Sparring. But without the gloves.

Another hour goes by, we end up with muscles sprained, twisted, and sore. Dripping sweat again.

"Mark my words, that hit is going to cost you," Corvidus told me, sternly.

"Really? What can you possibly do?"

"You have no idea what I can do."

"Let's see about that." I grinned.

"Okay. Enough."

"What?"

"Next," Corvidus was breathing heavily,

"is training in your dragon form."

"I'm not ready for that."

"You'd better be."

I turned around and sighed.

The sooner we kill his father, the sooner we kill him.

I turned again. "Fine." I say and I remove my amulet and drop it to the ground. I suddenly grow and grow and grow. In my dragon form, I release a huff of smoke. He yells to me so he can be heard, "Try whatever you can do. Try breathing fire."

I breathe louder, as if I were telling him "how?"

"Just concentrate. Think of fire. And then open your mouth. It should work, like last time, remember?" He winked.

It worked.

Within seconds of doing what he said, I was able to breathe fire. It was glittery forest green. I almost set the trees on fire. Luckily, I aimed higher, toward the sky. After doing something that came to me so naturally, as though I have been a dragon all along, the next step was uncovering my other powers.

I had a theory. What if since I was a dragon now, I could see far away?

Maybe 'zoom in'? After all, I am a predatory species. Maybe I'd have this power that could help me see far away.

I attempted it. Just focus, Freya…

I focused on people walking a far distance away, through the forest. And somehow, I just told my mind, "Zoom in."

And it did exactly that.

I could see the natives of Evermist walking with much clarity, and in fact, when I tried to hear what they were saying, that worked too!

I had special hearing and seeing abilities. Cool!

I felt so drained of energy by the time I uncovered these powers that I felt the need to turn back into my human form.

I grabbed the amulet which was on the ground and held it within my claws.

I turned back into a human. Wait, am I still human? I don't even know at this point.

Almost immediately, my body falls and collapses to the ground.

Corvidus comes rushing to my side and places a hand on my back.

He sighs, "Yeah, I think it's time to show you the cabin."

"What cabin?"

He grinned and grabbed my hand. Then we disappeared and reappeared just after a few seconds into a warm, cozy cabin. I could smell the burned cedar from the fireplace and feel the warmth of the fire encompassing the entire area.

He lifted me up and helped me walk to the nearest bed and placed me on top of the sheets. Corvidus folded over the blanket and told me to get some sleep.

"I'll be back tomorrow, try not to burn someone to a crisp before I'm back."

I smiled, "Oh, I won't. I'm saving all that energy for burning you."

He laughed and then said, "I'm heading back to Zantedeschia. I thought it'd be nice for you to have some privacy."

"Oh my god, Who are you and where's Corvidus, what have you done with him?"

"Nice try, but this is just more solid proof that you care about me."

I sighed and then finally said, "Bye!" as a signal for him to leave.

He understood and then started walking and disappeared into thin air again.

I started having second thoughts about killing him.

*Maybe he's not so bad after all?*

# Chapter 15

# Oh, Chris

I woke up at around eight in the morning the next day and brewed a cup of tea while waiting for Corvidus to arrive. As I was making my tea, he suddenly appeared through a tornado of ravens in the kitchen and he made me drop my mug.

"Jesus! Knock much?" I said to him in anger. But then his tone grew deep as he told me, "We need to talk. It's important."

I dropped everything that I was doing and walked up to him and said, "Tell me," as I looked him in the eyes.

We went to my room and sat on the bed. He started talking after taking a few deep breaths.

"My father is dead."

"WHAT?"

"Murders have happened in Alexandrite Academy and my father... is dead."

"What? Ho- Who?"

"Christopher is the main suspect as of now."

I immediately stood up in rage.

"Could Chris really have done this?"

"He's behind bars right now. His magic has been restrained."

"No. No. NO! That's crazy! But is it though? I don't know who to trust or what to believe!"

"I'm sorry."

"I want to see him. NOW."

"No. This is insane! You're putting yourself at risk!"

"He's my friend. I need to see him, Corvidus."

Corvidus nodded and told me that he'll take me, but only after informing me about a million times that it was dangerous to see him.

I responded with, "I can fly there in my dragon form. It's easier than your wormhole, raven cyclone scenario."

"Okay. But please, please be careful. I can't come with you; I can't enter Viridesca, remember?"

I nodded and then left to step outside so I could transform to go to Viridesca.

I took off my amulet and held it in my hand and turned into a dragon. I started flying upwards so I could see where I was heading better.

I saw Viridesca's palace and aimed toward the large crystal forest just outside Emeralda. I held my amulet and thought of turning back into a human, and I did.

I sprinted inside the castle, hoping to find someone who could explain what was going on.

Heading toward the castle dungeons, I saw a couple of Viridescan guards standing outside a cell. I neared the cell and saw Christopher.

"Chris! What the hell happened?"

"Freya? Freya! How are you here? I've been worried sick about you!"

"Stop. Just Stop. Tell me the truth, did you kill those people at Alexandrite? Did you kill Locke?"

"No. I didn't." Christopher spoke with an eerie, low voice. Straightforward, demanding.

Then one of the guards looked at me and said, "Excuse me, who do you think you are? Storming in here to talk to a prisoner?"

I told him I was Christopher's friend and said I needed only 2 minutes to talk to him. The guard looked at me and left.

Immediately, I knew not to believe Chris. But either way I said, "I believe you."

I knew something was wrong; I just couldn't point my finger at what it was. I knew he would only kill when it came to me or his family. It's not right. *It's not right, it's not right, it's not right* was all I could think about.

CHAPTER 16

# Axel's Return

After speaking with Christopher, I left Viridesca and flew back to Evermist. I enjoyed the sights of the forests while flying and even took the time to truly feel myself in my dragon form. This was me. I had to learn to accept all of me, no matter how I looked or which creature I was. And I truly started feeling free. I returned to Evermist's cabin and saw Corvidus swinging himself on the swing just outside the cabin. I walked up to him and said, "Thank you for letting me see Chris."

"Sure, not like you'd let me tell you otherwise." He raised an eyebrow at me while fidgeting with his nails.

"I'm famished. Anything to eat?" I walked into the cabin's kitchen.

He followed me silently, and as I saw what was inside the kitchen, he grinned. There was a table full of plates and bowls of fruits, salads, sandwiches, and fries. My stomach started grumbling as I took in the sight of what lay in front of me.

I picked up a sandwich and sat down at the table. "Do you really think Christopher killed your father?"

"I don't know what to think..." He didn't talk for the next two minutes, after which he said, "Freya, we need to talk..."

"I don't care, I'm not talking to you unless I need to." I was looking at him with all seriousness.

"I'm sorry."

"Like I said, I don't care."

"You don't know the pain I've been through, honestly, what is it you humans call? When we sit with another human, and we talk out all our feelings to a professional?"

"You mean therapy?" I smirked.

"Yeah! Yes, that!"

"You are too late."

"What does that mean?"

A pause.

"Therapy only works with those who are willing to face their fears, insecurities, and traumas as soon as possible. If what you are saying is true and you have some unresolved trauma issues, you're too goddamn late."

"Oh."

He kept looking at me but didn't say anything.

"I see my reflection in your eyes. I hope I'm not wrong." I turned to look at him.

"Because if I can be fixed, so can you, Corvidus. And it starts with fixing your mistakes, starting with me."

There were a few minutes of awkward silence which went by, after which I continued talking. I asked Corvidus if he'd let me go now that his father was dead...

"Absolutely not."

"What the hell?"

Silence.

"This wasn't our deal."

"The terms of our deal have changed; there's been an external factor involved."

"It can't change without you consulting me first!"

"Oh yes, it can!"

"Why won't you let me go? Didn't we just talk about fixing your mistak—"

"Because I want to rule Zantedeschia with yo—"

***Creak.***

THUD.

The door of the cabin fell down.

I heard footsteps nearing the kitchen, I went to Corvidus' side, afraid of whom it could be or what it could be.

"Freya? Are you here?"

I stood up.

**"Axel?"**

**"Freya!"**

"Oh my god! I've been so worried!"

"Me too! I was looking all over the place for you, there have been search parties everywhere trying to find you!"

"I'm so sorry! Corvidus, he took me!"

"This guy?!" Axel pointed at Corvidus.

"Well yeah, bu—"

<u>PUNCH. HIT. SMACK.</u>

"Whoa, whoa, whoa. Stop!"

Corvidus looked at me with a black eye."What the hell Freya?!"

"I'm sorry, wait, Stop. Axel!"

He finally finished beating up Corvidus.

Just as he turned to talk to me, though, Corvidus hit him with a punch.

"Hell. Guys! Stop!"

They finally stopped hitting each other, and then both of them looked at me. They had bruises all over themselves.

I burst out laughing.

"You think this is funny?" Corvidus stared at me.

"Umm **yeah?**"

They were not amused.

"Who the hell are you, man?" Axel asked Corvidus.

"Prince of Zantedeschia. Corvidus Locke. And who might you be?"

"Wait, if your father's dead. Aren't you technically king?" I asked.

"I suppose so." Corvidus replied.

"Axel Aretos, her—"

Pause. He turned to look at me before saying

"—friend."

"It's not okay for you to just kidnap her when she's in the process of becoming her dragon form."

"Hey!" I interrupted.

"It's not okay for him to kidnap me like EVER. Not just in that scenario."

"And it's okay for you to abuse people in front of a lady?"

"What?" I stared at Corvidus and asked him how he knew. "Besides, didn't you abuse me too?" They continued fighting.

"GUYS! Just stop arguing. There's no point. You've both made mistakes. Just leave it at that."

"Go back to Alexandrite Academy, I'll be there to collect you later, after which you can rule Zantedeschia with me as Queen." Corvidus stared at me and gave me an order.

"Hey! I'm not some item for you to just collect! And what if I don't want to rule Zantedeschia with you?"

"We'll see. To both those things." He says and teleports out of Evermist using his raven cyclone.

"Let's go, Freya. I'll protect you. At least **someone** cares about you," Axel states confidently, grabs my hand, and we step outside the cabin, ready to go back to Alexandrite Academy.

While walking outside, I asked Axel, blushing, "You care about me?"

He just cleared his throat and looked down.

CHAPTER 17

# Six Feet Under Silas + Crowning Ceremony

Axel decided to return to Alexandrite Academy the same way he came, a helicopter.

And I decided that I wanted to clear my mind some more, so I would return as a dragon. After all, mostly everybody knew about my transformation.

So I finally landed on the field as a dragon, huffing glittery, forest green fire.

As I did so, I saw many people clapping for me. I felt proud of myself, but little did they know I was still bound in servitude to Corvidus. Clearly, my life was taking different turns than expected. After turning back into my, well, normal, human self, I went into my dorm room to see my friends, Dara, Michelle, and Taylor. They welcomed me back with hugs and kisses.

"We missed you! We were so worried, but Axel told us that he'd find you and bring you back safely, one way or another."

I nodded.

"I guess he did it," Taylor said.

After settling down for a bit and doing some light reading, I decided to go for a swim. We usually have underwater swimming training and practice on Tuesdays, and that day was a Thursday, but nevertheless, I was still craving the water, so I packed up my swimsuit and headed to the indoor pool at around 6 pm.

As I was swimming, I noticed a shadow above the water, but I didn't think too much of it; I'm used to 'seeing things,' as one would say.

But unfortunately, since I didn't react, I later came to know that trouble was headed my way.

I saw a contoured male face just above the edge of the pool, and as I came closer to investigate, I was pushed deep into the pool, and my face was held there.

I was drowning.

I couldn't breathe in my state of panic, and also because, well, you know, I was UNDER WATER. I finally channeled my dragon side in pain and, as a human, breathed fire.

The fire was so strong that I started to see the male's face being burned, and he screamed in pain. I was finally able to breathe, and I jumped out of the water.

I saw one of my worst enemies at Alexandrite Academy standing there, incinerated. Silas.

He was dead.

*Jeez,* I'd never killed anyone before, especially not a student. Well, this sure was going to cause problems. After getting out of the pool and taking a quick shower, I went to the principal and told her what happened. She started blaming me.

"Would you not be careful? Why did you even burn him? You're supposed to be normal, Freya! Everyone already sees you as a threat; this will definitely throw them off.

I tried explaining to her the situation, but to no avail.

Somehow, some time went by, and I returned to the field. That was when Corvidus reappeared in a cyclone of ravens and grabbed me.

We reappeared a second later in Zantedeschia's Castle.

"Not again!" I ground my teeth.

He grinned.

"Corvidus! Axel doesn't know where I am! We have to go back!"

He shook his head no.

Corvidus led me to what was supposedly 'my' room and told me to get ready for the crowning ceremony. He would be declared King, and me, Queen. I didn't want this; I didn't ask for this. I tried to convince him to let me go, but he just wouldn't budge.

I went into my room and came back out a couple of minutes later, readily accepting my fate since Corvidus wouldn't give me an option.

Proceeding this, the crowning ceremony happened. I was crowned Queen, and Corvidus was crowned King, since Locke, his father was dead. That meant the legacy moved on to him. And now, apparently, me.

Suddenly, we heard screeching noises coming from outside. We ran outside just in time to see a horde of dragons flying in the sky, a group of pitch black and bright gold. We were shocked to our cores. It was assumed that I was the only dragon alive. But before we could discuss much, one particular dragon came really close to me and grabbed me in its talons and claws, and I was taken away.

CHAPTER 18

# My true family

The dragons took me to a secluded forest, and they transformed into humans. I saw my true family. I had never felt such a sense of belonging as I did then. I felt at *home*.

I saw a woman running to me and hugging me, along with a man doing the same.

"We're your parents, Freya."

I started crying, tears streaming down my face as I said, "It's about time."

We all hugged tightly, and they started explaining why they left me.

"We just wanted a normal life for you, Freya. We knew that dragons were hated in the fae world. We made you become a changeling for this precise reason. We had no idea your adoptive parents would treat you the way they have. We're truly sorry."

"If it helps, I wouldn't have found you if I didn't have abusive parents."

"We hope you'll forgive us?"

"Of course, I do! You're my real parents!"

I ran to hug them.

"Shall we introduce you to our friends and relatives?" My parents asked me with eager curiosity.

"YEAH?!"

After a while, I helped make bonfires and tents in the forest. My parents explained to me that they keep living in the wilderness because it's what their hearts crave, and it helps them shift into their dragon form whenever they like. They also have to be on the move continuously because of the fact that they might be caught. And apparently, things do not go well if they're caught. Dragons are disliked more than feared among the Fae community.

In the process of making friends, I asked questions to find out how dragons existed and how the color is chosen for each dragon's fire, scales, etc., and what powers we have, etc. I also got some time in to ask why they took me away during the crowning ceremony.

They said, "We did that for two reasons. 1, to reunite you with us, your true family, and 2, to warn you."

"What did you want to warn me about?"

"Corvidus is the good one, Christopher is not."

It took a minute from my side to let that sink in. When I asked them to explain themselves, they didn't. That's just it. There's no more to it. I was so angry. How could they say Chris was bad? He literally took care of me for so long! I was confused. Startled, in fact. I didn't know who to trust.

CHAPTER 19

# Grand Entrance

A few days in, I finally settled in with my family pretty well. We continued to stay in tents, making it easier to transform and fly whenever necessary. My family had lived like this, always on the run and hiding, for a long time.

But something started to feel suspicious, and I realized that they had been avoiding telling me who Christopher and Corvidus really were.

Suddenly, during breakfast, I saw a large green crystal erupting from the ground, shaped in the form of a throne, and sitting on it was Christopher.

"Hello Freya, love."

"Chris! How did you get out of the—"

"Unnecessary information."

"How are all of you?" Christopher stalked toward my parents.

I then saw them trembling and shaking, and I immediately got worried.

"I'm still won—"

I stopped him. "Wait. Are you by any chance mad at me, for, you know, not getting you out of the dunge—"

"Nonsense! Water under the bridge!" He said, stepping closer to me.

"Okay…?"

He then started talking to my parents. "I'm going to need to bunk with you all for a couple of weeks."

Chris turned to look at me and said, "I want to know more about Freya's lineage. After all, she still needs protection from Corvidus. Who knows when that creep can show up? Am I right?" He started laughing.

I noticed my parents' movement around him was very limited; they barely said a word since he got there. Something was wrong. And whatever my parents did, every other human-dragon followed.

"Hey, I need to talk to you alone," Christopher grabbed my arm and rushed me into a tent.

"Why are they trembling?" He asked me with a stern look in his eyes.

"Umm, I don't know..." At the sound of his voice, I started trembling too.

"Freya!" He yelled right in my face.

I whispered, "They're afraid of you!"

"What?!"

"Yes. They're scared!"

"Freya, you KNOW me, you have to trust me, I didn't do anything!"

"SHH. I believe you. I think?"

"Thank you."

A few weeks went by, Chris stayed with me, and I tried convincing my parents and the others that Christopher is good and has done nothing bad. They don't speak, not a word since he arrived.

I decided that I was going to return with Christopher back to Viridesca. All of this because he was telling me that my family was going to betray me soon. I don't know what made me believe him. In fact, I didn't even ask questions or demand proof. But one thing I did know was that I felt really drawn to Chris. Something about him was just magnetic. But I felt like I was not in control of my feelings and emotions. I was drawn to him, but I didn't necessarily want to be drawn to him. I can't exactly explain it. It was weird. This insane feeling of trust brewed in me, and I didn't know where it came from. It was just something I felt.

Anyways, I really did trust him, even if that meant I was going to leave my family behind. But if he was right, then I wasn't really missing out on much. Besides, he's been there for me since day one, so I left without saying anything to my family.

That day, Chris and I reunited in an amazing way! We planned to go horse riding through the woods.

"All ready?" Chris asked me.

"Yep."

"Here, let me give you a boost." I blushed. Till this day, I don't know why.

"You excited?"

"Hell, yes!"

We went off into the woods, galloping away, happily ever after.

The end.

Haha, got you again. Just kidding!

Okay, in all seriousness though, let's continue the story.

"Be careful over that rock!"

THUMP.

I fell off my horse and onto the soily, muddy ground.

"Okay, Upsy daisy." Chris helped me up and healed me with his magic.

"Shall we head back to the castle?"

"Sure?"

We headed back to the castle, and darkness had fallen by the time we got back.

Christopher brewed me some matcha milk, and it helped me sleep.

"Freya?"

"Hmm?"

"Just so you know, I'll do anything to protect you."

"Yeah?"

"I mean, as long as you're wearing that amulet and you're in this castle, no harm will come to you."

"Thanks, Chris, for everything."

After sleeping for some time, I woke up in the middle of the night feeling sick to my stomach.

I asked Chris if it had something to do with my dinner or even the milk.

"No, I mean, I don't think so. Our kitchen is incredibly clean and sanitary, and there's no chance for any food poisoning to happen."

"What- *gags* what was in the milk?"

"Just Matcha and Turmeric."

I tilted my head at him, and that was when he gave me this evil smirk.

I was concerned for myself.

My eyes turned purple and started to glow. I felt incredibly angry. Rage built a home inside of me.

"Come on, let's get some fresh air…" Chris guided me outside.

## CHAPTER 20

# Surprise

I started throwing around whatever was near me and inside the castle on my way outside. Something had really built up this anger in me.

My eyes started stinging and glowing an even brighter purple color.

As soon as Chris brings me outside, I fell to the ground, I yelled out a screech of pain, and suddenly transformed into a dragon, even while wearing my amulet.

The force and pressure were so much that the amulet snapped in half!

"Now!" I heard Chris yelling, and I turned behind me in my dragon form to see a cage falling over me.

"Finally!"

I roared out in pain, but not in physical pain, in emotional pain.

He—He captured me.

CHAPTER 21

# Axel + Corvidus >>>

Christopher started laughing - no - cackling, as he said, "They were right! Your parents? I'm the bad one!"

I let out another roar in anger.

So it was, in fact, the milk/dinner, I guessed.

"I was the one who eradicated all dragons from the fae world. Don't get me wrong, I was genuinely planning to help you, until I figured out you were a dragon!"

I let out a hiss as though I was cursing at him.

Suddenly, I saw Axel and Corvidus appear, flying on one of my dragon relatives/parents.

They started shooting at Chris with a gun. *Where in hell did they get a gun?*

I let out another hiss and fell to the ground in a loud THUD.

Eventually, though, my anger took over, and I broke free from the cage with my strength and flames.

I escaped and found my way to fly to Zantedeschia.

I ended up crying there, even in my dragon form, and noticed that dragon tears were more like diamonds. I mean, I guess, Amethysts in my case.

I just ended up waiting for Axel and Corvidus to return.

The night went by while I was alone and wondering where Axel and Corvidus were.

I'm still a dragon, yes, I haven't found a way to turn back into human without my amulet. So yes, it's been a tough night.

What you don't know is, the night got tougher.

I heard skittering and screeching coming from within the Zantedeschian forest.

I immediately knew what was going on. Fleskies. The damned creatures were after me.

I end up seeing Fleski in the distance, and as they come nearer, I used the opportunity of me being a dragon to my advantage and ended up burning all the Fleski alive.

I somehow found time to sleep and found a spot just behind this one pine tree and slept, again, still in my dragon form, waiting for Axel and Corvidus to arrive.

Morning eventually comes, and I found Axel and Corvidus waiting for me right near the Zantedeschian castle. They chucked a brand new amulet at me, and I immediately held it tight between my talons and turned back into my human, disheveled form.

I immediately ran to hug them.

I hugged them tight and started crying.

"Umm, what do we do in situations like this?" Corvidus asked Axel, to which he replied, "Do I look like I know that answer?" I started laughing and hugged them again, wiping my tears.

"Thank you."

"Don't go getting all mushy on me. We hate each other, remember?" Corvidus clicked his tongue.

"Oh, I remember alright!"

I slapped Corvidus. "That's for the Scelena."

I punched him next. "That's for my family."

But then I grabbed him and planted a kiss on his cheek and Axel's. "But this is for saving me and caring about me even though you guys don't act like it." I winked.

# Chapter 22
# Family Time

My family found me in Zantedeschia and brought my friends from Alexandrite Academy along.

We all decided to have a feast to celebrate escaping Christopher and talked about our strategies for defeating him.

"Freya, Christopher isn't dead," Axel told me.

"What do you mean?" I asked.

"Well, we hurt him, that's for sure, but he has some of the strongest magical healing powers in history," Corvidus stated.

"What do you think we should do now?"

"We know that Chris won't come after you for a while since we're all here for you, and his body has been severely damaged."

"There's not much to worry about, at least not for now. So for the time being, let's just enjoy our victories, shall we?" My father told me.

We ended the day by bursting firecrackers and concluding the feast with pictures, videos, cake, and, of course, more firecrackers.

This was my story.

And it was just the beginning.

# LIMITED EDITION VERSION:

## Chapter 22

# Corvidus' POV

I looked at her with awe. I kept looking at her. I think I was falling.

Before I could explain to myself that vulnerability is risky and not the right step ahead, my heart jumped faster than my brain ever could into the river of love. And I was swimming, drowning in it. I wondered what Axel thought of her. Freya. I felt horrible. Torturing her, taking her, she wasn't mine to keep, no matter how I felt.

This was her story, and I was the villain in it. Or was I?

She forgave me too easily, I felt.

I didn't deserve her.

But where was all this coming from? I hated her. Hell, I was the one who insisted on the torturing. Clearly, I must be mad. If my emotions can go from despising to loving so easily…there must be something wrong with me.

But I'm happy.

I haven't been happy in a long time that I almost forgot how it felt to be happy.

She made me happy.

And I was the villain in her story.

Not Christopher, not Axel, but me.

I was the villain in **her** goddamn story.

THE END

# Acknowledgments

First off, I would like to thank Sarah J Maas for being a lifelong inspiration and for writing "A Court of Thorns and Roses," "Crescent City," and "Throne of Glass." These books have always been my best friends and have given me exactly the right amount of courage, strength, and motivation to finish this novella. I highly recommend these fantasy books to anyone who hasn't read them.

Secondly, I would like to thank Rebecca Yarros for her book "Fourth Wing".

Many thanks to my wonderful and supportive parents and my dog, Milo.

A special thank you to my sister, Gayatri Balachandar, who read the very first few pieces of my writing and gave me her honest input when I just started working on this novella.

Thank you to Sara Lubratt (you can find her on YouTube). You really helped me during those days when I felt I couldn't get my creative juices flowing, and whenever I reached out to your YouTube channel, I got just what I needed. I was never disappointed.

And finally, thank you to my English teacher, Ms. Athira TP who has always given me words of encouragement, praised me, supported me, and inspired me to another level altogether.

Thank you all. I wouldn't be here without each and every one of you.

www.ingramcontent.com/pod-product-compliance
Lightning Source LLC
LaVergne TN
LVHW041214150826
845673LV00001B/397

* 9 7 9 8 8 9 1 3 3 9 9 3 4 *